R

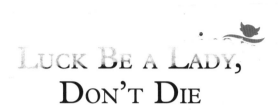

Luck Be a Lady, Don't Die

LUCK BE A LADY, DON'T DIE

ROBERT J. RANDISI

THORNDIKE
CHIVERS

This Large Print edition is published by Thorndike Press, Waterville, Maine, USA and by BBC Audiobooks Ltd, Bath, England.

Thorndike Press, a part of Gale, Cengage Learning.

Copyright © 2007 by Robert J. Randisi.

A Rat Pack Mystery.

The moral right of the author has been asserted.

The text of this Large Print edition is unabridged.

Other aspects of the book may vary from the original edition.

Set in 16 pt. Plantin.

Printed on permanent paper.

LIBRARY OF CONGRESS CATALOGING-IN-PUBLICATION DATA

Randisi, Robert J.
   Luck be a lady, don't die / by Robert J. Randisi.
      p. cm. — (Thorndike Press large print mystery)
   "A Rat Pack Mystery"—T.p. verso.
   Includes bibliographical references.
   ISBN-13: 978-1-4104-0494-7 (hardcover : alk. paper)
   ISBN-10: 1-4104-0494-3 (hardcover : alk. paper)
   1. Rat Pack (Entertainers) — Fiction. 2. Entertainers —
Fiction. 3. Gangsters — Fiction. 4. Casinos — Fiction. 5. Las
Vegas (Nev.) — Fiction. 6. Large type books. I. Title.
PS3568.A53L83 2008
813'.54—dc22   2007046299

BRITISH LIBRARY CATALOGUING-IN-PUBLICATION DATA AVAILABLE

Published in 2008 in the U.S. by arrangement with St. Martin's Press, LLC.

Published in 2008 in the U.K. by arrangement with the author.

U.K. Hardcover: 978-1-405-64464-8 (Chivers Large Print)

U.K. Softcover: 978-1-405-64465-5 (Camden Large Print)

Printed in the United States of America
1 2 3 4 5 6 7 12 11 10 09 08

*For Marthayn, who has been
my Lady Luck
for almost fifteen years*

PROLOGUE

May 20, 1998
The chairman was dead.

Frank Sinatra had been known by many names over the years. "Frankie" when he was wowing the bobby-soxers in his younger days, "Has Been" before he appeared as Maggio in *From Here to Eternity* and blew that label all to hell. He was christened "Chairman of the Board" when he founded the Reprise record label in 1961, and forever was referred to as "Ol' Blue Eyes."

I called him my friend.

The funeral service at Good Shepherd Catholic Church in Beverly Hills was by invitation only. I had one in my pocket. That was how I knew I wasn't the only one who thought that he and I were friends.

The stars had come out to say good-bye to Frank. From my vantage point I could see Kirk Douglas, Robert Wagner, Jack Lemmon, Johnny Carson, Anthony Quinn,

Tony Curtis and Bob Dylan. Marlo Thomas was there. It was the second funeral in that church I knew of for her. Danny Thomas' funeral had been held there seven years before.

The celebrities I knew well enough to speak to because they had played the Sands in Vegas a time or two were the likes of Jerry Lewis, Tony Bennett, Milton Berle, Debbie Reynolds and Liza Minelli. Steve and Eydie waved at me from across the room. Bob Newhart and Don Rickles were sitting together with their wives and nodded. Angie Dickinson even waved. I was seventy-eight that year. I didn't know how old Angie was, but she still did it for me. She smiled and I remembered that day in 1960 when Frank finally introduced us.

The family was seated in the front row. Frank's wife Barbara, his daughters Nancy and Tina, and his son Frank Jr. In the row directly behind them sat Frank's two surviving ex-wives, Mia Farrow and Nancy, who had her hand on Junior's shoulder.

Another row back were the surviving wives of Rat Pack members, Dean's ex-wife Jeannie, and Sammy's widow Altovise. Of all the wives, former wives and widows, I only knew Jeannie, slightly.

I doubted either of my ex-wives would attend my funeral, unless it was to make sure I was dead. The wife attendance was proof that if they didn't love Frank Sinatra, most of Hollywood certainly respected him. And then, of course, there were those who just wanted to be seen at his funeral.

It was part funeral part vigil, actually. The street outside was crowded with Frank's fans, and his longtime pianist, Bill Miller, had played "In the Wee Small Hours of the Morning" and "All the Way" as we filed into the church. Just a few days ago, the day after Frank's death, I had been in Vegas when all the lights — and I mean *all* the lights — on the strip were dimmed in his honor.

Even though I was familiar with most of the people there that day, and not particularly awestruck since I'd met many of them before, I was looking at Sophia Loren — who also did it for me. Trying not to gape at her ageless, legendary beauty I was startled when somebody said in my ear, "Hey, Eddie G."

I looked up and saw Joey Bishop leaning over me.

"Jesus, Joey." I got up and he hugged me. He felt brittle. I wondered if I felt the same way. Two old men, old friends, trying not to squeeze each other too hard.

"Ain't seen you in a dog's age," Joey said.

"What've you been doin'?"

"Not much. After they blew the old place up two years ago I just didn't have it in me to work anywhere else. So I retired." I didn't bother to tell him that no one in Vegas had room for a septuagenarian pit boss.

"You're goin' bald," he said.

"And you're gray."

He laughed shortly, but it didn't make it to his sad eyes.

"I'll see you later, Clyde," he said, squeezing my arm before moving on. "Clyde" was Rat Pack talk. Shirley MacLaine was there. She and Angie were sort of mascots, but Joey was the last of the five. It made me sad. I remembered all of them — Frank, Sammy, Dean, Joey, even Peter, who I didn't care for that much — as vital, young guys back in 1960.

I shook hands with Wayne Newton and Paul Anka before sitting back down for the service. Cardinal Roger Mahony eulogized Frank and I could hear people around me crying, some quietly, some sobbing hysterically. I hadn't cried since the dust from the old Sands got in my eyes the day of its implosion, but I found myself fighting tears back. If I cried it wouldn't only be for my dead friend, but also for all the lost years. I hated to think it and even more to say it,

10

but as I got older I knew that the 60s in Vegas had been the best years of my life, and the Rat Pack was a big part of that. I don't think any of us went on to be happier. Perhaps some of us rose to greater heights — Dean, with his hit movies and his wonderful TV career — but none of us were, I think, ever happier.

The Cardinal droned — as is usually the way at those things — so I just closed my eyes and drifted back in time. . . .

ONE

Las Vegas,
July 30, 1960
"The idea is to hang out together, find fun
with broads, and have a great time. We
gotta make pictures people enjoy."
— Frank Sinatra

Sometimes they scream, thinking you'll feel
sorry for them. Then the first break comes.
Crack! Audible, like a branch snapping.
That's when they start yelling that they'll
never cheat again.

"Not in my casino, anyway," Jack Entratter said.

They get no sympathy from Jack. He's had
lots of bones broken for him over the years,
and some he even broke himself.

They get no sympathy from me, either,
especially not when I'm the one who caught
them at it. I get pissed when some smart-
ass tries to cheat at one of my tables. Even

13

from my position in the pit I could spot this one a mile off. You can't nick the corner of a card without me hearing it, and this guy was clumsy about it. Plus, he stood out in his Nehru jacket and beads. Both might have been popular for the time, but they were not normal blackjack table attire.

"Boss?" one of Entratter's men asked.

Jack thought about it while the two hoods held the cheater down. He gave it some serious consideration and then said, "Break one more."

"Which one?" the hood asked.

"You're a leg-breaker," Entratter said. "Figure it out." He looked at me. "Let's get out of here."

We left the back room and walked down a hall that would take us back to the casino floor of the Sands. We could still hear the cheater yelling.

"The guys are comin' back ya know."

"I heard," I said. The "guys" he was talking about were the Rat Pack: Frank, Sammy, Joey Bishop and Peter Lawford. Dean was already playing the Copa Room.

"From Dean?"

"No," I said, "I haven't seen Dean . . . yet."

"He's been here a few days," Jack said. "After you bailed him out last time you ain't heard from him?"

"No. I guess he's been busy."

We reached the casino floor and Jack stopped. For a moment we both absorbed the sounds — the dice, the roulette wheel, the voices. This was home to both of us.

"Want me to talk to him?" he asked.

"No, Jack," I said. "If Dean wants to see me he'll say so."

"Okay." He slapped me on the shoulder. He was a big man and sometimes forgot it. He almost knocked me over. "Good job spottin' that guy."

"Yeah. Thanks."

"But a helluva way to start a day, huh? I'll see you later."

We split up there, Jack heading for his office and me back to the pit — only I detoured and went into the Silver Queen Lounge for a drink first.

It was quite a change, from the back room with broken bones to the casino floor with its lights and bells, cards and broken hearts.

I sat at the bar and waved Harry over.

"Heard you caught a cheater," he said.

"Bourbon, ice."

He pulled a face. "Musta been a bad one."

"Just another loser sent to the hospital," I said when he brought my bourbon.

"Then why the drink in the middle of the day?"

I stared at him.

"I have to explain to you why I want a drink in the middle of the afternoon?"

"Jeez, Eddie," Harry said. "No, ya don't."

He walked away, dragging his bruised feelings with him. I didn't feel bad about the kid with the broken arm and — I assumed, after we left — leg, but I felt bad about busting Harry.

That's when I realized I had some bruised feelings of my own. All it took was Jack asking about Dean and the guys. After I helped Frank and Dean out when they were in Vegas in February shooting *Ocean's 11*, I guess I kidded myself that we were friends. Now they were coming back to town for the opening of the film at the Fremont Theatre. I thought maybe, with Dean getting there first to play the Copa Room, I'd hear from him, and then from Frank when he hit town. But why would a couple of big timers like Frank Sinatra and Dean Martin want to be friends with a pit boss from Brooklyn? They had left Vegas six months ago and probably forgot about me a week later. I stared at the mural behind the bar. It ran the length of the bar, had been painted by an artist named Allan Stewart, and depicted the history of Vegas from the gold rush days to the exploding of the atom bomb. Finally, I pushed the half full glass away. I was acting like a snubbed broad, getting my feelings hurt and all. Stupid.

"Harry!"

"Yeah?" He came over.

"I'm sorry I snapped at you," I said. "Bad day." I dropped a fin on him as a tip.

"Hey, no problem Eddie. Thanks."

I looked around.

"Bev's not here?"

"Come in tonight. I thought you and her was done?" he said, then backed off like I was going to snap his head off again.

"On and off," I said. "Like I am with most broads."

"I hear ya," he said. "I ain't found one worth all my time yet, either."

I didn't bother telling him that Beverly Carter was worth my time, she just deserved better than me.

I knocked on the bar and said, "See you later."

"Sure."

I left the lounge and went back to my pit, where another boss was covering for me. Jack Entratter had a rule for his staff. If you caught somebody cheating you had to follow through all the way and watch them pay for it. I had started spotting cheaters as a dealer, and never flinched the first few times I had to follow through. Jack liked that and eventually bumped me up to pit boss because of it.

"Bad?" Leo Goldman asked as I joined him in the pit.

"Bad enough," I said. "He won't cheat again — at least, not here. And it'll be a while before he can do it anywhere, again."

"You back?" Leo asked.

"I'm back," I said. "Go on, get out of here."

"See you tomorrow."

I waved and went to work, watching the tables. A pit boss has to watch everything, not only the players but the dealers, too. And God help the dealer who got caught cheating in Jack Entratter's Sands. I'd followed through on a cheating dealer once, and I never wanted to do that again.

TWO

When I saw Joey Bishop coming across the floor toward me it took me back six months to the first time I'd gotten involved with the Rat Pack as something other than a fan. Meeting Frank and especially Dean had been a thrill for me, and being able to help them, even more. Six months of silence, however, had taken the shine off of it. As Joey got closer, smiled and waved, my stomach did a flip-flop. I didn't know if I was pissed, or excited.

"Hey, Eddie G!" he greeted me, enthusiastically.

"Joey." We shook hands. "I didn't know you were in town already."

"I came ahead to, you know, get everything in order for the Leader."

"How is Frank?"

"Ah, ya know," Joey said. "He's been moonin' over Ava again lately."

"I thought he was seeing Juliet Prowse?"

"He is," Joey said, "but you know how Frank feels about Ava."

Well, yeah, I did, but it wasn't by hearing it from Frank. It was from reading the gossip columns, like every other Clyde.

"Anyway," Joey said, "I got a message for you."

"From Frank?"

"Naw," he said, "from Dean. He's playin' the Copa, you know."

"Yeah, I know. I can read a marquee."

Joey eyed me for a minute, then said, "Dean would like to see you."

"Where?"

"He's on the golf course."

"Now?" I asked, annoyed at the tone of my own voice. "I can't right now, I'm workin'."

"I'm sure Jack would let you go to see Dean," Joey said.

My boss, Jack Entratter, would pay me extra to keep guys like Frank and Dean happy.

"Okay," I said, finally, "tell Dean I'll be there."

"Great. There's a car waitin' for you outside." Joey slapped me on the arm. "Good to see you again, Eddie."

"Yeah, you too, Joey."

As I watched him walk away I wondered

when I had gotten so predictable?

It was just at the start of my shift, so I had somebody cover for me again. Entratter would have wanted me to go right up as soon as Joey gave me the word. He considered these guys his friends — especially Frank — and wanted them kept happy when they were in "his joint." All of us knew that was part of the job. Even when Dean decided he wanted to deal blackjack and paid off a good-looking broad who got twenty-two, Entratter wouldn't squawk.

I went out front and found a limo sitting there waiting for me. The driver jumped out and opened the door for me. When I got in I found myself staring at a monolith with legs named Mack Gray. Gray used to be George Raft's Man Friday but when Raft fell on hard times and couldn't afford him he "gave" him to Dean Martin. Our first meeting had not gone well, and the way he was staring at me I wasn't sure this one was going to go any better.

"Hey, Mr. G.," he said, sticking out his hand. "How ya doin'?"

Apparently, Mack remembered that I had covered for him last time and probably kept him from losing his job — and going to jail.

"Hey, Mack," I said, shaking his hand.

21

"Good to see you."

"The boss is waitin' for ya." At that moment the limo jerked, and then started moving.

"Any idea what this is about, Mack?"

"That's for the boss to tell you."

Dean had left Mack in the dark last time, which had hurt the big guy's feelings and led to all the trouble. It was my guess that Dean had filled him in this time, and he was just being tight-lipped.

We didn't have far to go, just down the strip, because Dean was playing at the Desert Inn Golf Club, a course that had opened in 1952.

The limo pulled us in close to the greens, and not the clubhouse. As Mack and I got out he checked his watch.

"The boss should be on the eighth hole by now." He looked at me. "There are clubs and shoes in the trunk for you."

"That's okay," I said. "I don't play."

He just shrugged.

We walked a few feet to a golf cart, which barely fit the two of us. Mack drove, and because of his bulk every time he executed a turn I had the feeling I was going to be thrown.

We drove across green grass and over some hills and finally came within sight of the eighth hole. Mack's estimate was correct. Dean and another man were about to tee off, their caddies standing off to one side. They stopped when they saw us coming, and waited for us to reach them.

As I got out of the golf cart, Dean walked over with his hand out. He was wearing tan slacks and a light blue polo shirt with a white collar. No argyle golf beanie for Dino. The other man however, was decked out in plaid pants and a matching beanie.

"Eddie, how the hell are you?"

"Good, Dean, I'm fine," I said, as he pumped my hand.

"Fine? If I was you I wouldn't be fine, I'd be pissed." He looked over his shoulder at Mack, who remained in the cart. "Think he's pissed, Killer?" "Killer" was Mack's nickname left over from his days in boxing.

"I think so, Boss."

"Pissed?" I asked.

"You must've heard I was in town," Dean said, "playing the Copa, and I hadn't called you yet. We're friends, right?"

"Well . . . I thought so —"

"Don't think, Eddie," Dean said, grabbing my shoulder. "After what you did for me, we're friends."

I didn't point out that it was he who had probably saved my life — and Bev's — in the Sands parking lot. That would have put a different slant on the moment.

"I've just been caught up with work, you know? And family stuff. And we got this premier comin' up."

"And the Cal Neva," Mack reminded him.

"Right," Dean said, flinging his arms. "Frank and I bought into this casino in Tahoe, but I'm gettin' out. I don't like bein' in so tight with the boys, you know?"

I knew. Frank was from Jersey and Dean from Ohio, but it was Dean who had dealt with mafia types his whole life. He was not as impressed with them as Frank was.

"Anyway, I asked you up here so I could apologize, and give you these."

He brought his hand out of his pocket and offered me two tickets. I accepted them and saw that they were for the special performance down on Fremont Street. The movie was included.

"Thanks, Dean."

"Bring that beautiful redhead you were with the last time we were here," Dean said, "or whoever your lady of the moment is."

"I will," I said, without specifying which.

He looked me over.

"You're not dressed for golf."

"I don't play, Dean."

"Then I won't make you follow me all

24

over the golf course. We'll go to the club and I'll buy you a drink." He turned and called to the other man. "Bob, I've got to go. Thanks for the eight holes."

The man waved and said, "See you, Dino." He looked up and flashed a famous grin.

"Mack," Dean said, "I'll drive. You can walk back, can't you?"

"Sure, Boss."

"Come on, Eddie."

We got into the cart and he executed an expert turn and headed us back to the club.

"He's gonna play his eighteen holes," he said, about the other player. "Seven was more than enough for me today."

"Dean?"

"Yeah?"

"Was that Bob Hope?"

He looked at me and smiled.

"Yeah, Eddie, that was Bob Hope."

We each ordered a bourbon when we got to the bar in the clubhouse. Celebrities were not news there, and no one really fawned over Dean. And while my contacts stretched from the highest rollers in the casinos to the lowest denizens of the streets, I didn't know anyone in this club. This may have been the only place on Vegas where I was out of my element.

25

The bartender said, "Here's your drink, Mr. Martin," when he put the glass down, but that was it.

We drank and talked, caught up a bit. He told me stuff you couldn't find in Hedda Hopper's column, things about his family, his films, his albums. He had done an album of Italian songs that he thought was horrible, the reasons having nothing to do with his voice, which was still as smooth as silk.

By the time he finished Mack Gray had joined us, looking flushed and sweaty. I had the feeling Dean had been killing time until Mack got there. He got a cold drink from the bartender, cleared his throat and said, "Boss?"

"Yeah, Mack?"

"Ain't you gonna ask 'im?"

"Ask him what?" Dean turned and looked at the big man.

"You know . . . about helpin' out?"

"I can't do that, Mack," Dean said. "I don't want Eddie to think that's the only reason I asked him here."

I didn't know if they had worked out this song and dance routine before I got there, or if Dean was being sincere.

"What's the problem?" I asked.

Dean looked at me. I thought he appeared conflicted and I preferred to think he was being sincere.

"It's not my problem, really," he said, finally. "It's Frank's."

"Is Frank in town?"

Dean nodded and said, "He got here today, on the q.t. Nobody knows. Sammy and Peter are here, also."

"How did they manage that?" I asked.

"Limos, tinted windows, a few bucks spread around," Dean said.

"So what's Frank's problem?"

"That would probably be better coming from him," Dean said. "Only he doesn't really want to talk about it."

"He doesn't want help?"

"Oh, sure," Dean said, "but he doesn't want to ask. Does that make sense to you?"

"Only because I know Frank."

"Yes, you do," Dean said, "or you wouldn't understand. I tell you what. I'll leave a couple of tickets at the Copa for you for tonight's show. After it's over, come backstage. Maybe he'll talk to you then."

The first time I'd met the Rat Pack it'd been Frank enlisting me to help Dean. Now it was the other way around. I drained my drink and put the glass down.

"Okay," I said. "I'll be there."

Dean walked me to the door, his arm

27

around my shoulder, Mack trailing behind us.

"I mean it, Eddie," he said. "I asked you here to apologize and give you those theater tickets. But it occurs to me that you could be a big help to Frank. I'm not trying to manipulate you."

"I know that, Dean."

"If you can help Frank, I'd be grateful, and I know he would be, too."

"Well," I said, "let's see if he'll let me."

Dean slapped me on the back and said, "I think I'll join Bob for his last few holes."

I looked past him and said, "See you, Mack."

"S'long, Mr. G."

It didn't matter that I had saved Mack's ass last time. In fact, maybe he liked me even less for that. But he was being courteous.

I rode back to the Sands in the limo alone thinking — foolishly or not — that I was once again "in."

THREE

After Dean sang "That's Amore," he surprised everyone in the room — except me — by bringing Frank, Sammy, Joey and Peter on stage. From that point on it was another Summit Meeting, the Rat Pack at their best, interrupting each other, never finishing a song or joke, bowing to all the applause and hugging each other before they left the stage.

I hadn't brought anyone with me, the extra ticket still tucked away in my pocket. I'd told Harry the bartender that Bev and I were on again, off again, but we'd been sort of off again, off again for a while, now. I still thought she was beautiful, a great gal, and believe me, I was never being modest when I said she deserved better. Actually, it was me pointing out that fact once too often that had been the last straw for her.

"Call me," she said, without anger, "when

you decide that you *are* good enough for me."

So I was alone as I worked my way through the crowds to the stage where a couple of the Pack's bodyguards recognized me and passed me through.

Backstage was a madhouse, but most of the mob was made up of civilians out in the halls, not celebrities in the dressing rooms. Somehow, the boys had managed to keep it a secret that they were in town. The crowd was mostly hangers-on, and not A-types. If the word had gotten out, believe me, Buddy Hackett, Rickles, Nat King Cole, they all would have been there. The other reason it was easy to tell they'd kept the secret was that there weren't that many babes back there. Oh, Dean brought the women in, all right, but add Frank to that — and maybe even Peter — and the broads would have been beating down the doors. Even though, at that moment, Frank was the only Rat Pack member who was not married.

There were bodyguards in the back as well, manning the doors, but I knew one of them and he let me pass. I found myself in Sammy's dressing room, not Frank's.

"Oh, sorry," I said, "I was looking for Frank."

"Next door," Sammy said, then frowned.

"Hey, I know you, don't I?"

"Eddie Gianelli," I said. "I'm a pit boss here at the Sands."

He snapped his fingers.

"You're the cat who was askin' all the questions last time, right?"

"That was me."

"You know," he said, standing up from his makeup table. If anything he seemed smaller than I remembered, but Sammy Davis commanded respect, even with his tux half on and half off. The force of his personality filled the room. "I found out what that was all about later. You coulda told me, man."

"It wasn't my place, Mr. Davis —"

"Sam," he said, "just call me Sam."

"Sam, it wasn't my place to tell you anything. That was up to Frank and Dean."

"I dig where you're comin' from," Sammy said. "You really helped Dean out. You're a cool cat. I remember."

"Thanks."

"Frank's in the room next door," he said, "on the right. You comin' out with us tonight? We're gonna blow off some steam."

"I, uh —"

"In case you didn't recognize it, man," Sammy said, "that was an invitation."

"Thanks, Sam," I said. "I'll, uh, think about it."

31

"Do that, man. Let Frank know." He sat back down in his chair, continued removing his makeup.

I left his dressing room, moved one down and got the okay to enter. I knocked this time, anyway.

"Who is it?"

"Frank it's Eddie," I said, wondering if he'd remember, "you know? Eddie Gian—"

"Eddie G!" he shouted. "Get your ass in here, son!"

I felt foolishly pleased.

He met me at the door and was pumping my hand even before I had closed it behind me.

"What the hell, pally," he said. "You don't call, you don't write . . . not been a postcard. I thought we were friends."

I was stunned. Could it really be that he had expected me to call him? Keep in touch?

"Gee, Frank, I'm sorry —"

"Hey," he said, "we're all busy, right? We got lives?" He slapped me on the back, then turned and walked back to his makeup table. He was still wearing his shirt, but open to expose his bony chest, and his tuxedo pants. The suspenders were hanging down loose. He was wearing a pair of soft slippers.

"You saw the show?"

"I saw it."

"You got tipped, right? That we'd all be here?"

"Dean told me," I said. "He gave me a ticket."

Frank paused, turned in his chair and stared at me.

"Dean told you?"

"That's right."

"What else did he tell you?"

"Not much," I replied. "Only that you might have a problem you needed help with."

We looked at each other for a few moments and I couldn't gauge his reaction. Was he going to be pissed at Dean?

Then he said, "That Dean," and a look of affection came over him. "Whatta guy, huh? He knows somethin's wrong but he don't know what, yet he still sends you in. Eddie G. The first team. Whatta pal."

"Hey," I said, "you did it for him last time, right?"

"That I did, buddy boy, that I did," Frank said. "Only this time, I don't know if you can help me, Eddie." He turned and looked into his mirror. "Or more to the point, I don't know if you'll want to once you find out who and what's involved."

I didn't like the sound of that but I said,

33

"I guess I'll have to be the judge of that. Right, Frank?"

FOUR

Frank wanted to talk, but he wanted to do it where we wouldn't be interrupted.

"Your place," he said. "If I remember right you make a good pot of coffee."

"If I remember right," I said, "you made the coffee."

"Oh, that's right," he said. "Well, do you have the same brand?"

"I think so."

"Good," he said, as if that settled it. "Your place."

So we went out the back where he had a limo. He gave the driver my address — I was surprised he remembered — and told him to take us to my house.

"What about the others?" I asked when we were under way. "Won't they wonder where you are?"

"I'll join them later," he said. "Hey, we got booze in here. You want some?"

"I don't think so."

He had a decanter of something in his hand, but put it down.

"Nah, me neither," he said. "I'll wait for the coffee. Or maybe there's some beer in this little refrigerator."

"I have a better idea. There's an all night Chock full o'Nuts just a block further up, on the right."

"You don't have Nedicks here, do you?" Frank asked. "I love Nedicks in New York. Hot dogs and orangeade really go down easy after a show at Radio City."

I couldn't believe one of the biggest swingers of the century was telling me how much he liked hot dogs and orangeade. Nedicks was actually one of the places I missed in New York. That and Nathan's.

"No Nedicks," I said, apologetically.

"Ah, Chock full o'Nuts sounds good. Henry!" he shouted. "About a half a block there's one. Stop there."

"Yes, Mr. Sinatra."

After the limo pulled up in front, Frank looked at me.

"Black, no sugar," I said.

He told Henry how we wanted our coffee. "Sure thing, Mr. Sinatra."

Six months ago Frank had appeared at my house late one night still in his tux, like now, with the tie loose. He looked totally relaxed.

"Maybe I should just go ahead and fill you in, huh?" he asked. "This is as good a place as any, right?"

"I guess so."

"This probably starts the way a lot of stories start," he said, "but there's this girl . . ."

"Juliet Prowse?"

"No," Frank said, "another girl."

"Judith —"

"Do you want me to tell it?" he asked.

"Okay, okay," I said, "sorry."

"I've been seeing her — you know — on the sly? We didn't want to show up in Hedda or Louella's column, you know?"

"Sure."

Henry returned and knocked on the window. Frank lowered it, accepted the coffees, and then told Henry to just drive around.

"No point going to your place for coffee now, right?" he asked, handing me a container.

"Right."

"You know," he said, as the car started forward, "I just read this piece in Hedda's column where she quotes Ava as saying what a sweet guy I was when I was down.

You know, before *From Here To Eternity*?
But that after I got back up on top I turned
into an arrogant shit."

"I, uh, didn't read that. Did Ava really say
that?"

"That's what Hedda claims," he replied,
"but whether she said it or not, Jesus . . . of
course I was sweet when I was down.
Nobody would give me the time of day.
What was I supposed to do, shoot myself?"

"No, of course not."

"You're damn right," he said, growing
more agitated. I knew Frank carried a gun,
had a permit for it. I wondered if he had it
on him. "And now they see me as arrogant
because I'm on top? Well, lemme tell you
Eddie, you don't stay on top by being Mr.
Nice Guy. You gotta be a prick to stay there,
and believe me, I been down and I never
want to go back there."

I didn't say what I was thinking, that there
were plenty of people on top who weren't
pricks, but I kept my mouth shut for two
reasons. One, I didn't see those people in
their everyday lives. How was I to know if
they were pricks or not?

The second reason was I still didn't know
if Frank was carrying his gun.

Frank sipped his coffee, took a deep

38

breath and said, "Okay, so there's this girl . . ."

FIVE

"Her name is Mary Clarke," Frank said. "Very simple and unassuming, just like her. You don't need to know the whole story to help me. All you need to know is that she was going to meet me here."

"Here? In Las Vegas?"

"That's right."

"For the premiere?"

"Not exactly," he said. "She came because this is where I was, and we were going to meet . . . discreetly."

"Is she married?"

"No."

"Are you trying to keep this from Juliet?"

"Well . . . yeah, of course I don't want Juliet to know."

"But that's not the real reason you're being discreet," I said.

"No."

I studied him for a moment, then asked,

"This is the part I'm not gonna like, isn't it?"

"Well, yeah."

I took a sip of my coffee, wishing it was bourbon. I looked longingly at the glass decanter Frank had picked up when we first got into the car.

"All right, let me have the bad news."

"It's really not all that bad," Frank said, "because I can handle MoMo."

"MoMo?"

"That's right."

"As in . . . MoMo Giancana?"

"Right."

"This Mary Clarke . . . she's Sam Giancana's girl?" I asked with a dry mouth.

"He thinks she is."

"That's the same thing, Frank," I said. "When the Boss of all Bosses thinks a girl is his, she's usually his."

"Don't blow it out of proportion, Eddie," Frank scolded me. "I told you, I can handle MoMo."

"Jesus . . ."

"After all," Frank went on, "he didn't mind sharing Judy."

"Judy . . . Campbell?"

"That's right."

"Judy Campbell is MoMo's girl, too?"

"She was," Frank said, "before she went

41

on to JFK."

"Wait a minute," I said, "I slept with the same girl who slept with Sam Giancana and John F. Kennedy?"

He frowned and said, "Apparently we both did."

Now I wondered if Frank was going to get all bent out of shape because Judith Campbell ended up in my bed after a party in his suite six months ago.

"Frank, listen —"

"Don't worry about it, Eddie," Frank said. "Judy's out of the picture as far as I'm concerned."

"But Mary Clarke . . ."

"Very much in the picture . . . at least, she was supposed to be."

"So what happened?"

"I don't know," Frank said. "That's what I need you to find out."

"She's missing?"

"She was supposed to be here to meet me, and she's not."

"So maybe she never got to Vegas," I said. "Where does she live?"

"Chicago," Frank said, "but she was here. I spoke to her on the phone two days ago. She said she was here waiting for me."

"Where?" I asked. "I mean, what hotel?"

"The Nugget, downtown."

"Is that smart, Frank?" I asked. "Having her in the Golden Nugget, right on Fremont Street? Near the theater?"

He scratched his head.

"Well, I thought it was better than having her here on the strip at the Flamingo, or the Riv," he said, "but now that you mention it, maybe that wasn't such a good idea . . . but that's where you're gonna have to start."

"Have you been there lookin' for her?"

"I told you, we're tryin' to be discreet," he reminded me. "I called lookin' for her, but she doesn't answer."

"But they have her registered?"

"That's what they said."

I stared out the window at the scenery going by. I could see that Henry was driving in circles.

"Listen," Frank said, tapping me on the knee, "this wasn't my idea, remember? You don't have to say yes."

"I don't see the harm in me . . . poking around a bit. I mean, I don't have to get involved with Giancana." I looked at him. "Do I?"

"Of course not. MoMo's not in Vegas, and Mary saw to it that he wouldn't be expecting to see her for a while."

"What'd she tell him?"

"That she had to go and sit with a sick friend."

Christ, I thought.

"Yeah, I know," Frank said, reading my mind, "but she's a sweet kid. It's exactly the kind of thing she'd really do."

"Do you have a picture of her?"

"I figured you'd be needing one."

He took a snapshot out of his pocket. She was a dish, all right. The color photo showed her blond hair and a well-endowed figure wrapped in a pink sweater. That was all I could see, but I was willing to bet the legs matched.

"Can I take this?"

"If you're gonna be lookin' for her? Sure. I got others."

"Okay," I said, taking the photo, "okay, Frank. Let me see what I can find out."

He slapped me on the back with more strength than I thought him capable of.

"I knew I could count on Eddie G," he exclaimed. "Dino suggested I ask you and I said no. I didn't wanna get you involved. But he was right. You've got this whole town wired. You'll find her. I've got faith in you."

"If she's even in town."

"She's here," he said. "She's here and my buddy Eddie will find her. Henry, take us

44

back to the Sands."

"Yes, Mr. Sinatra."

Six

When we got back to the Sands Henry dropped us at a back door and we split up. Frank went to his suite and I went looking for Jack Entratter. It was late and he wasn't in his office. Neither was his girl, but she kept regular hours and Jack didn't. I found him wandering the casino, eyeing the punters, keeping watch for any more cheaters. I thought maybe he hadn't had his fill of breaking bones, then immediately told myself that wasn't fair to him. He had people to report to who would break *his* bones if they thought he wasn't doing the job he was being paid to do.

"Hey, Eddie," he said, his face lighting up when he saw me. "Heard you went to the show tonight."

"I did."

"Bet you weren't surprised, huh?"

"No, I had warning," I said. "Jack we gotta talk."

"Casino business, pal? Or personal?"

"A little of both, since it involves your buddy Frank."

"Let's go into the lounge," he said. "I could use a drink."

I never saw anybody more uncomfortable in expensive suits than Jack Entratter. Because of his size he always looked like he was going to burst out of them.

When we got to the Silver Queen I headed for the bar but he said, "Let's get a table. It's more private."

It might have been more private but it also meant that Bev was going to wait on us. When she came over she smiled at us both — I think.

"What can I get for you gentlemen?"

"Hello, sweetie," Jack said. "Scotch for me, rocks."

"Yes, sir, Mr. Entratter. Eddie?"

"A beer, Bev."

"What kind?"

"Anything on tap will do."

"Coming up."

As she walked to the bar Jack watched her ass all the way.

"Weren't you tappin' that for a while, Eddie?" he asked.

"I'm not here to talk about my love life, Jack," I said, sourly.

"Sorry," Entratter said, "didn't mean to hit a nerve. Okay, then, what's on yer mind?"

I told him about seeing Dino on the golf course, going to the show, to Frank's dressing room, and then about our ride around town.

"Okay," he said, leaning back as Bev set down our drinks, "you told me everything but what Frank wants you to do."

"Jack . . ."

He held up a big hand. "You'll leave that to Frank to tell me if he wants me to know, right?"

"Hey, you're the one who wants these guys kept happy while they're here."

"I know, I know." He picked up his drink and downed half of it. "So what you're tellin' me is you need to be off the clock to do somethin' for Frank, right?"

"Right."

"Okay, kid, you're off." He finished his drink. "You gonna drink that?"

"Slowly."

"I'll see you around, then." He stood up, towered over me. "Keep me posted, okay?"

"You know I will."

"No, I damn well don't know you will," he said, "that's why I'm tellin' you."

"All right, all right," I said, "I'll keep you

posted."

I don't know why I decided to drink my beer slow. Maybe it was so it wouldn't look like I was running out, trying to avoid Beverly. I sipped it and she stayed away, even though she didn't have many customers. She stood, talking to the bartender, waiting for somebody — one of her three patrons — to order another drink. I didn't want a second one and neither did the couple who was arguing at another table. They were young, probably on their honeymoon, and she was reading him the riot act about losing more than twenty dollars at the slot machines. Used to be only the broads worked the slots, but lately I was noticing some men playing them, too.

Finally I finished and decided to brave the lioness in her den.

I got up and walked over to where she was standing. Bev didn't have showgirl looks, but that was only because she was too full bodied. She had the rack for it, but she also had the thighs and butt to go with them. Not for the stage but just right for other things.

Her red hair was piled up on top of her head tonight, but her green eyes were not sparkling at me the way they had in the past. Her kissable mouth was set hard, disap-

49

pointed.

"Finished, Eddie?" she asked.

"Yes." I reached into my pocket.

"You know Mr. Entratter doesn't get charged for drinks, right?"

"I know it," I said. I dropped a fin onto her tray, as a tip.

"Gee, thanks, Eddie."

"Bev . . . how are you doin'?"

"Me? I'm fine. How are you?"

"Um, pretty good. I, uh —"

"Eddie," she said, "you don't have to make nice to me, you know."

"Bev, I'm just trying to be . . . friends."

"We are friends, Eddie," she said. "No more than that. You made it clear."

"Bev —"

"I have work to do." She picked up her tray, then stopped and put her hand on my arm. "Really, Eddie . . . it's fine."

She walked away to check on her other customers. I looked at the bartender, a guy named Leon, who just gave me a sympathetic shrug.

I did the same, then turned and left.

Seven

It was late — but the word "late" is relative in Las Vegas. It wasn't too late to gamble, see a show, get something to eat or get laid. It was, however, too late to go down to the Golden Nugget and question the hotel staff about a guest. Those kind of questions were better asked during regular hotel hours. So I left the bar with nothing to do but go home.

I went into the parking lot and got into my '53 Caddy. I'd had a '52, which I had driven from New York to Vegas, but somebody blew it up trying to kill me six months ago, the last time I tried to help Frank and Dean. I hoped this time trying to help them out would not cost me another car — or worse.

When I pulled into the driveway of my little house I turned off the motor but remained behind the wheel. Once again I was thinking about last time, when two men had attacked me in my home. I waited for my eyes to adjust to the shadows my house threw, then got out of the car and walked carefully to the front door. Nobody jumped me and pushed me inside, but even before I unlocked the door and opened it I could smell it.

Coffee.

Somebody was in my house, and they had made coffee.

I entered and closed the door softly behind me. In a corner behind the door I had secreted a Louisville Slugger. It had been there for six months and this was the first time I'd picked it up.

Carrying it in both hands, I moved quietly through the living room toward the kitchen. I could hear someone moving around in there. It could have been Frank, though I doubted it. It could have been an old girlfriend, but I couldn't remember ever having chosen a broad because she could make coffee, and the aroma was pretty good.

The kitchen had a swinging door. I stopped just on my side of it and listened. Somebody's feet were scuffling around my kitchen, as if they were preparing more than just coffee. I decided to just go ahead and take the plunge.

Holding the bat in my best Mickey Mantle

grip — even down to the little finger hanging over off the knob — I rushed through the swinging door, scaring the crap out of two people.

One of them was me.

The other was a big Jewish enforcer from New York named Jerry Epstein.

"Jesus Christ, Mr. G.," he said, staring at me. "You scared the shit outta me!"

He didn't look scared, standing there holding my coffeepot in one hand and a sandwich in the other. He hadn't dropped either one.

"You want a sandwich?" he asked. "I made two."

"You were expecting me?" I asked. "Now?"

"Naw," he said, "If you didn't come in the next ten minutes I was gonna eat the other one."

I lowered my bat. Jerry was in shirtsleeves, and under his arm in a shoulder rig was a huge .45. If he'd been there to whack me my baseball bat wouldn't have done much good. Luckily, we were friends . . . kinda.

"Jerry . . . what the hell are you doin' here?"

"Same as last time, Mr. G.," he said, walking to the kitchen table. "Watching your ass."

"On whose say so? Frank's?"

"Actually, it wasn't Mr. S. who called me, it was Dino. Called earlier today and told me you'd need some help to help Mr. S. I caught the first flight out, got in late, thought I'd come right here."

Calling Dean "Dino" was as much a sign of respect to Jerry as calling Frank "Mr. S."

So Dean had called Jerry right after we spoke. I guess he assumed Frank would go ahead and accept my help.

Jerry sat down, poured himself a cup of coffee and bit into his sandwich.

"How'd you get in here?"

He licked a glob of mayonnaise from the corner of his mouth and said, "A door ain't hard ta open, Mr. G."

"Jerry . . ."

"Yeah?"

Last time out, Jerry had not only been a big help, he'd saved my life. I could bitch about being predictable, but I couldn't bitch that he was here.

"I'm glad to see you," I finished.

"I'm glad ta see you, too, Mr. G.," he said. "I been meanin' ta come back to Vegas, ya know, just to gamble and shit . . . and ta see you, of course. I just been kinda busy, ya know?"

"I know, Jerry," I said. "Believe me, I know."

"Ya want that other sandwich?" he asked. "It's ham and cheese."

I looked over at the food on the counter, then walked to the drainboard to retrieve my coffee cup. I grabbed the sandwich and joined him at the table.

"There's no mayo on this one, is there?" I asked.

"Naw, not yet," he said. "I woulda put it if I was gonna eat it."

I poured myself a cup of coffee and bit into the sandwich. Ham, Cheese, lettuce on white bread. All I ever had was white bread.

"Hey, wait," I said.

"What?"

"There's mayo on yours?"

"Yeah, so?"

"I don't keep the stuff in the house, Jerry," I said. "Where'd you get mayo?"

Looking sheepish he admitted, "I brung my own."

"You carry your own mayo?"

He nodded.

"And mustard. Last time I was here I went through your cabinets and saw you didn't have any. I hope you ain't mad."

"How can I be mad, Jerry?" I asked. "I like a man who comes prepared. Mayo,

55

mustard, and your forty-five."

He smiled and took another big bite out of his sandwich, dripping mayo onto the table.

EIGHT

Funny, I woke in the morning a little pissed. I would have preferred Jerry to show up the next day, after I had agreed to help Frank. It was like the more I thought about it through the night the more it upset me that I was so predictable that Dino sent for him before we even spoke.

Of course, none of that was Jerry's fault. He slept on the couch, and when I woke I could smell bacon and coffee. I'd forgotten about the benefits of having him around, other than saving my life.

" 'Mornin', Mr. G.," he said as I entered the kitchen. I'd pulled on a pair of slacks and a t-shirt. He was still wearing the trousers from a gray suit and his white shirt, although it was unbuttoned, showing an expanse of the whitest skin I'd ever seen, beneath a mat of chest hair.

"Jerry, you think you can call me Eddie, instead of Mr. G.?"

He handed me a cup of coffee, thought about the question, then said, "I don't think so, Mr. G."

"Just thought I'd ask."

He put a plate of bacon and eggs on the table with some toast — perfectly golden, though I'll never know how he did that in my toaster — and sat down across from me.

"You ain't got any orange juice."

"I'll pick some up today."

"So," he asked, "what do we gotta do?"

"Dean didn't tell you?"

"All Dino told me was that I was supposed ta keep you safe."

"Well . . ." I thought it over quickly and decided to play straight with him. "We're looking for a girl."

"What girl?"

"Just a girl." Well, maybe not completely straight. "She's supposed to be stayin' at the Golden Nugget, but nobody's seen her in a couple of days."

"Then I guess we gotta go there and look, right?"

"Right."

"Where is the Golden Nugget?"

"Down on Fremont Street."

He stared at me blankly, chewing a huge mouthful of food.

"The street where we went that time you

had pancakes . . . at the Horseshoe . . . with my friend Danny Bardini?"

"Oh, the P.I.?"

"Right."

"Those were good pancakes," he said. "Can we go there again?"

"Sure."

"We gonna see that guy, again? The P.I.?"

"Probably," I said, "but I think we'll snoop around on our own first."

"Okay with me," Jerry said, "but he was okay, that guy."

"Yeah, he was."

We finished breakfast and Jerry insisted on cleaning the kitchen. I left him to do that while I showered and dressed. When I came back downstairs he was ready. He was wearing the same wrinkled gray suit. I had on a windbreaker and blue jeans, taking a break from my everyday black suit.

"Jerry, where's your suitcase?"

"Dino got me a room at the Sands. It's there."

"We'll have to get you some fresh clothes."

"Don't worry," he said. "I wear the same clothes a lot."

"Still, at some point we'll go to the Sands so you can change, maybe pick up your suitcase."

"Whatever you say, Mr. G."

When we stepped outside he said, "I noticed you replaced your Caddy."

"Kinda."

"This is a fifty-three, right?"

"Right," I said. "Good eye, Jerry."

"Can I drive it?"

Nobody had driven this Caddy but me since I got it five months ago, but I remembered how well Jerry had handled my old one.

"You, me and nobody else," I said, handing him the keys.

NINE

The Golden Nugget — along with the Horseshoe — was the gem of Fremont Street. That might have explained why Frank put Mary Clarke there.

As we drove past the Fremont Street Theater Jerry asked, "Are you goin' ta the openin', Mr. G.?"

"I've got a couple of tickets."

"Takin' that good lookin' waitress you was seein' last time I was here?"

"Uh, no, things have changed, we're not, uh, seeing each other, anymore."

"Hey, too bad," he said. "She was a sweet kid."

"Yeah, she was," I said, then corrected myself. "I mean, she still is."

Jerry took his eyes off the road for a second to look at me.

"Sounds like maybe you're still stuck on her."

"It wouldn't matter, Jerry," I said. "She's

not stuck on me."

"Like you said," he replied, "things change."

I directed Jerry to park behind the Nugget and we went in the back way. While I wanted to talk to the hotel staff — particularly the front desk people — there was someone else I wanted to see first.

"Hey, whoa," Jerry said as we reached the door of the office I wanted. "A cop?"

I looked at the letters, which spelled out HOTEL SECURITY.

"Not a cop, Jerry. A house dick."

"A dick's a dick, Mr. G.," he said. "They make me nervous. If ya don't mind I'll wait out here."

"Suit yourself," I told him. "I can't get in any trouble in there, anyway."

I opened the door and went in without knocking. Dave Lewis was sitting behind his desk, crumpling up paper and tossing it into a wastebasket across the office — or trying to. The floor around the basket was littered with his misses.

"That's why the Golden Nugget pays you the big bucks," I said, startling him.

He turned in his chair and gaped at me, then relaxed when he realized I wasn't somebody who could fire him.

"Scared me outta a year's growth, Eddie,"

he said, "ya mutt. How you doin'?"

"Pretty good, Dave."

He stood up and we shook hands. He had a wad of paper in his left hand. All ready to go.

"Wanna give it a go?" he asked.

I snatched the paper from his hand and tossed it at the basket in one motion. It hit the rim and bounced away.

"I never could shoot hoops."

"Me, neither." He sat down in his chair, leaned back and looked up at me. He'd started out at the bottom, at the Nugget ten years earlier when he first came to town, had worked his way up to his own office. But the effort seemed to have aged him twenty years instead of ten. He was balding and had the potbelly of a fifty-year-old.

"What brings you down here?" he asked. "Entratter get smart and can your ass, finally?"

"No, I've still got him fooled. I'm lookin' for somebody who's supposed to be registered here."

"Supposed to be?"

"Well, she is, but I hear nobody's seen her for a while."

"Her? This some broad you're tryin' to hide out here, Eddie?"

63

"Just a nice girl who might be in trouble, Dave."

He sat forward in his chair, grabbed a pen and pulled a pad of paper over.

"What's her name?"

"Mary Clarke."

"What room is she in?"

"I don't know," I said. "I came straight to you, Dave. I haven't gone to the desk, yet."

"Okay." He tore the sheet off the pad and stood up. "Lemme see what I can find out. Wait here."

"Thanks." As he started for the door I said, "If you see a big guy in a wrinkled suit in the hall, he's with me."

"Why's he in the hall?"

"He doesn't like coppers, not even the hotel type."

"Can't blame him," he said. "Don't like them much myself. Sit tight, Eddie."

He left the door open behind him. I heard him stop short outside, probably at the sight of Jerry. A moment later Jerry stuck his head in.

"Where's he goin'?"

"To get us some information," I said. "Come on in. He's okay."

"What did he mean?"

"About what?"

Jerry came into the room.

"He said you was right about my suit."

"Oh, that," I answered. "I told him it was gray."

TEN

Jerry and I talked about the Caddy until Dave came back and closed the door.

"Decided to come in?" he said to Jerry, who didn't answer.

"This is my friend Jerry," I said. "Jerry, this is Dave."

"A pleasure," Dave said.

"Hey," was all he got from Jerry.

"Well," Dave said, "your girl checked in two nights ago and nobody's seen her since. She ain't been in any of the restaurants, and she ain't had room service. You wanna see her room?"

"That'd be great, Dave. Thanks."

"Let's go. Bring your friend."

We followed him to the main elevators and he took us up to one of the higher floors, where the suites were.

"Whoever's payin' her bill ain't cheap," Dave said, as we walked down the hall. He had a house key, but he didn't use it right away. He knocked first, waited, knocked a second time, then slid the key into the lock.

Dave was right. Frank hadn't scrimped on Mary Clarke's room. It was one of the best, with a view of the desert for privacy.

Jerry looked around. He didn't say anything but I could see he was impressed. The suite was at least the size of the one Dean Martin had at the Sands.

"How many bedrooms?" I asked Dave.

"Only one, but it's a big one, with a sunken bed."

"Can I look around?"

"Ya want some privacy?" he asked. "Just pull the door closed when you leave and come back downstairs if ya need anything else."

"I'll let you know when we're done," I promised.

"Come down to the office or just dial nine-two."

"Thanks again, Dave."

"Guy on the desk said this girl was a knockout. Young, blonde, big knockers, kinda dumb." Dave shrugged. "Sounds like every broad who comes to Vegas to me. But hey, to each his own. Good luck findin' her for whoever she belongs to." He looked at Jerry. "Nice meetin' ya, big guy."

"Likewise."

Dave left, pulling the door tightly shut behind him.

"I'm going to look around," I said.

"Want me ta do anything?"

"No. Just sit tight. If I knew what I was looking for, I'd let you help me. Why don't you have a drink?"

He looked over at the bar.

"I'm gonna be drivin' your Caddy," he said. "Maybe they got a coke."

I took a quick look around the huge room we were in, but there was nothing to even indicate that anyone had used it. I went down the hall next, to the bedroom and bathroom, and there I could see signs that a woman had used them. A suitcase was on the bed, open but still packed. Some toiletries were in the bathroom. Perfume, shampoo, comb, brush, hand mirror, nail stuff, she'd laid it all out. I went back to the suitcase and looked through it. She packed neatly: sweaters, blouses, skirts, a couple of pairs of slacks, and down beneath it all the lingerie. There were a couple of bras that told me she measured up to Jayne Mansfield or Mamie Van Doren pretty good. The entire suitcase smelled of her perfume. I didn't know if it had spilled in transit, or if it was just that strong.

I went through the suitcase a second time

and was glad I did. In the lining I found a photo of Frank. Not a stock photo, but one that, if anybody saw it, they would know that she knew him. It was inscribed — I couldn't read the handwriting — but I knew Frank's signature. I folded it up good and stuck it in my jacket pocket. I didn't know if her disappearance was going to end up a police matter. I was sure Frank would replace it. I'd apologize later.

I went over to the phone and dialed nine-two. Dave answered. I asked him if the girl had made any calls, or received any.

"She might have gotten a call, we can't tell," he said, "but we know she didn't make any long distance ones. Might've called someone local."

"Okay, thanks. We'll be out of here in about ten minutes."

"Find anything useful?"

"Well, her suitcase is on the bed and hasn't been completely unpacked. Was there any maid service up here?"

"Lemme check. Stay there until I call back."

By the time the phone rang I was sitting at the bar with Jerry. He was drinking a Coke. I didn't have anything.

"The maid went in but the bed hadn't been slept in and the towels hadn't been used. She said the suitcase was still on the bed."

"That was yesterday morning?"

"Right."

"Okay, Dave, thanks again. If I think of anything else I'll give you a call."

"Good luck."

Jerry finished his Coke, rinsed out the glass and put it back where he got it from behind the bar. I assumed the bottle was in the trash.

"We done?" he asked.

"We're done."

"Find anything?"

"Looks like she arrived, started to unpack, but something stopped her and she never got back to it. She never used the bed, and it looks like she never even came out here into this room."

"So whatta we do next?"

"I think we need a real detective."

"Your friend Bardini?"

I nodded.

"My friend Bardini."

ELEVEN

Luckily, the office of Bardini investigations was on Fremont Street, right between The Fremont Casino and Binion's Horseshoe, and above a gift shop. We walked down the block and stopped in front of the door marked 150.

"Wait, we gotta get some coffee and tea."

"Tea?"

"Penny — that's Danny's secretary — she drinks tea. I can't walk in empty-handed or she'll tear me a new one."

We went across the street, got three containers of coffee and one of tea, and then I led the way upstairs to the office.

When we walked in I was disappointed to see that Penny's desk was empty.

"She's not here."

"Too bad," Jerry said. "I wanted to see the broad who scares you so much."

"Danny's got to be in his office or the door woulda been locked." I left the tea on

71

her desk and walked past it to Danny's door.

"You in here?" I asked, opening it.

"Where else would I be?" he called back from behind his desk. When he saw Big Jerry behind me he said, "Yikes, the pancake man is back."

"Jerry's helping me with an . . . errand."

"An errand?" Danny asked. "For who?"

I didn't answer.

"Wait, don't tell me," he said. "I'm a detective, I've seen the posters and marquee down at the theater."

"Right."

He stood up and extended his hand to Jerry.

"Nice to see you, big guy."

"You, too," Jerry said. He shook hands then handed Danny a container. "One of these is for you."

"Thanks. My secretary is out today."

"Where *is* Penny?"

"Went to see her sister in L.A., so I'm manning the office alone. Pull up some chairs, guys, and tell me how I can help."

We each pulled a chair over, sat and took the tops off our coffee containers. Briefly, I told Danny who we were looking for and what we had done so far. He didn't interrupt, just listened.

"Okay," he said, when I was finished, "I'm

72

gonna assume that this is all on the q.t.,
right?"

"Definitely."

"And that Jerry knows everything?"

"Jerry knows what you know," I con-
firmed, which was also my way of telling
him that Jerry didn't know everything I
knew and that I'd fill him in later.

"Well, it sounds to me like you've done all
you can do," Danny said. "How well did
you search the room?"

"Uh, pretty well, I think —"

"Closets, cabinets, the bathtub?"

"Well, no . . . I didn't look in the closets
or the bathtub."

"I know Dave Lewis, too," he said. "I'll
get him to let me in. Maybe I can find
something you didn't. Talk to the parking
attendants?"

"No. I was going to do that next." Parking
attendants and valets were on my list. They
were part of my network and I knew at least
a few at each casino.

"I'll do it," he said. "They'll know if she
caught a cab or not."

I noticed Danny wasn't taking any notes.
He was good that way, had a memory any
cop would envy.

"When's the premier?" he asked.

"August third." Four days.

73

"We got until then?"

"At least."

"I better get on it." He stood up. "Got a picture?"

"Yeah," I said, "but only one."

"I'll take good care of it. I gotta have it to show around."

"Okay."

He looked at it, whistled and stuck it in his pocket. Jerry didn't see, or even try to.

"Am I gettin' paid for this?" Danny asked.

"I ain't," Jerry said.

"Me, neither," I said.

Danny shrugged.

"Just thought I'd ask."

"How about tickets to the movie and the show?" I asked.

"That'll do."

"Me, too," Jerry said.

"Well, of course, you too, Jerry," Danny said. "Eddie and I wouldn't go without you. What fun would that be?"

Jerry looked at me.

"Is he kiddin' me?"

"No, Jerry, he's not kidding," I said.

He'd thought Danny was pulling his leg and was about to get mad. Once I convinced him it was no joke he relaxed.

"Hey, Jerry," Danny said. "Relax man. We're all friends here, right?"

"Sure," Jerry said, eyeing Danny, "we're friends."

" 'Cause I'd sure hate to have you as an enemy, big guy."

Now Jerry smiled and it was scary.

"Yeah," he said, "you would."

TWELVE

Danny came down the stairs with us after locking his office. On the street he told me he'd get back to me as soon as he could, then he slapped Jerry on the back and took off in the direction of the Golden Nugget.

"Now what?" Jerry asked.

"Why don't we go to the Sands so you can change clothes?" I asked.

"Am I gonna be stayin' there or with you at your house?" he asked.

"Well, I don't really think there's any reason you have to stay with me, Jerry."

"You remember what happened last time?"

"That was . . . that was then, and this is now," I said, with a shudder because I did remember last time, very well. "None of that's gonna happen this time."

"Ya never know, Mr. G."

"Okay, we'll talk about it on the way."

We retrieved the Caddy and drove to the

Sands. I sent him up to his room to take a shower and get dressed, and to collect some clothes. We agreed that he'd keep some at my house, and some at the Sands, just in case. He said he had two bags with him, and he could pack one to take to my place.

While Jerry went to change I made my way over to Jack Entratter's office. I didn't know if he knew about Jerry or not, but I wanted to drop in and give him the word. Last time he'd had to get Jerry out of jail. I just thought he'd be interested to know the big guy was back.

Jack's girl let me go right into his office. From the look on his face he wasn't having a good day.

"Jack."

"Jesus Christ," he said, "don't tell me you have some bad news to add to my morning."

"I don't think so."

"Siddown!" he said, pointing to a chair. "I gotta bitch to somebody."

He went on to complain that three dealers were down with the flu, there was a flood on the second floor of the hotel, the kitchen did not get the shipment of steaks it was expecting . . .

". . . and the Gaming Board wants to see me tomorrow morning at eight a.m."

"What do they want?"

"What do they always want?" he asked. "They're lookin' for my license, *and* they wanna make me get up early. I don't need this when we're gettin' ready to renovate the rooms!"

He paused to take a breath, then grabbed a big Cuban and fired it up.

"What's on your mind?" he asked, his head ensconced in a cloud of smoke.

"I just thought you'd like to know that Jerry Epstein is in town."

"Epstein," he repeated. "Who's that?"

"You remember," I said, "he was here six months ago during the whole Dean Martin fiasco? You had to bail him out of jail?"

"That guy," Entratter said. "The big Jew from New York."

"That's him."

"Is he gonna help you with the new thing you're workin' on?"

"That's the idea."

He pointed a thick forefinger at me and said, "You better keep him outta trouble, Eddie."

"Jack, I don't have any control —"

"In fact, you guys better keep each other outta trouble," he said. "You've kept your nose clean since that whole magilla in February, but the Vegas cops don't like you so much."

"Hey, nothing that happened was my fault!"

"We know that," he said. "They're not so sure. So just don't find any bodies this time. And if you do . . ."

"Yeah?"

"Be smart and walk away."

I thought of several answers to that, but finally just said, "Okay."

"Is that big torpedo stayin' here?"

"Yeah, Dean got him a suite — but he doesn't like being called that."

"What? A torpedo? What is he, then?"

"It doesn't matter what he is," I said, getting up, "he just doesn't like being called that."

"Well, I'll have ta watch my fuckin' p's and q's around him, won't I?"

I didn't say anything. Entratter and Jerry were almost the same size, but Jerry was a lot younger. If push came to shove I'd have to take Jerry, so that sounded like a good idea to me.

"Now get outta here. I got work to do. This place is fuckin' fallin' apart."

Jerry was waiting for me down by the Silver Queen. He'd showered and changed, but he must have brought along some identical suits, because he looked the same, just without wrinkles. At his feet was a swollen duffle bag he had obviously stuffed with clothes.

"Place looks the same," he said.

"Yeah," I said, "not much has changed in six months."

"That redhead you like is workin'," he told me. "Stuck my head in the lounge to have a look."

"Uh-huh."

"You should talk ta her."

"Not right now, Jerry."

"She ain't busy —"

"It just wouldn't be a good time," I said, cutting him off, "believe me."

He shrugged. "Suit yerself. What are we doin' next?"

"I'm not sure," I said, "but my instructions are to stay out of trouble and not find any bodies."

"We can do that."

Not if our history was any indication.

THIRTEEN

I decided to let Jerry spend some time playing the horses. Our race book was located in a separate building and I left him there with the promise that I would not leave the casino without him. He was a regular at the track when he was in New York, and had impressed me last time with his handicapping ability. I figured he couldn't get into trouble while he was doing what he enjoyed.

I knew it wouldn't do me any good to try to find Frank, so I went in search of Joey Bishop. I probably could have asked Entratter to put me in touch with Sinatra, but if Frank had wanted Jack's help he would have asked for it. I decided to keep him out of it as long as I could.

During my search for Joey I had some celebrity sightings, which was not unusual in Vegas, or at the Sands, in particular.

I was about to walk past what would normally have been my station when John

Kelly, one of the newer pit bosses, waved and called me over.

"How're you doin', John?"

"Listen, I know you're off the clock and all," he said, which told me that word had gotten around, "but Vic Damone wants to raise the table limit."

"You know how Entratter feels about his showbiz pals, John," I said.

"Then I should do it?"

"How much does he want to play?"

"Ten thousand a hand."

"Sure," I said. "It's his money."

"Okay, Boss," he said, even though I wasn't technically his boss.

Vic Damone was headlining down the street at the Flamingo, but that afternoon he was playing blackjack in our place, which was what Entratter wanted. He didn't care where they performed, but he liked them to gamble at the Sands.

I also saw Danny Kaye shooting craps, figured he was in town for the opening of the movie. I waved and he waved back. Norman Fell and Buddy Lester, two of *Ocean's 11,* walked by me. I knew who they were but we really hadn't met formally. I started to wonder if Angie Dickinson was going to be in town. I had finally met her briefly toward the end of the filming back in February, but I knew if I had more time with her I could make her fall for me.

Yeah, right.

After about an hour I was starting to think that maybe I should ask Entratter to find Joey for me when I heard the comic's distinctive voice say, "You sonofagun," his signature line. I came around a corner and found him standing in front of a bank of slot machines with a group of older women who seemed to be mesmerized by him. As usual every hair was in place, and he was resplendent in a dark suit and a narrow dark tie over a white shirt. I always thought Joey did the most with what he had of anyone I knew. I also thought that if he heard me say that out loud he might not take it as a compliment, which it truly was.

"Eddie!" he said, with a big smile. He spread his hands. "Meet my fans."

The women all tittered, thanked Joey and moved on to put their nickels in the slots.

"That line always gets 'em," Joey said to me. "After Dean and Frank and even Peter, all I get are the old ladies, but I love 'em."

"What about Sammy?"

"Everybody loves Sammy," he said. "He's got the smallest body and the biggest talent, the sonofagun."

A middled-aged woman walking by put her hand over her mouth and started to laugh.

"See what I mean?"

"She wasn't so old," I said.

"Were you lookin' for me?" he asked.

"As a matter of fact, I was."

"But you're not lookin' for me, right? You wanna talk to the Leader."

"I do have to talk to Frank, yeah, Joey, but —"

He put his hand out and said, "Hey, don't worry about it. I know who my audience is, and I play to them."

"Everybody loves you, Joey. You're a funny man."

He slapped me on the back. "When do you want to see Frank?"

"Today, if I can."

"I'll talk to him. You gonna be around?"

"Yeah, I'll be here for a while."

"I'll see what I can." He closed his fist and tapped me on the jaw with it. "You sonofagun."

I couldn't help myself. I laughed.

FOURTEEN

I may have been off the clock but the fact that I was in the building meant people — like John Kelly — sought me out to ask questions. Most of the employees at the Sands thought I was more important than I was. Part of it was because I seemed to have Jack Entratter's ear, but I knew that another part was because I was thought of as being friends with Frank Sinatra, Dean Martin and other celebrities.

So I fielded some inquiries and handled them as best as I could. If it was something I couldn't answer, or a decision I couldn't make, I told them to call Jack Entratter, or to find their real boss. Some of the actual pit bosses they should have been reporting to, or floor managers, resented the amount of respect I seemed to get. That used to bother me, too, but eventually I figured it wasn't my problem, it was theirs, if they couldn't command the same level of regard, for some reason.

I was starting to wonder about Joey when he appeared, coming out of one of the elevators. He spotted me and waved and we met midfloor.

"Frank's in the steam, but he won't be there for long," he said.

"Does he want me to come down?"

"No," Joey said, "wait half an hour then go up to his suite."

I'd never been to Frank's suite. We'd always met in the steam, or in a limo. One time at my place and another on the set of the movie.

"You know where it is?"

"Yeah, I know," I said. "Thanks, Joey."

He looked past me and said, "I see some of the boys are here."

I thought he meant some of the "boys" but when I looked over my shoulder I saw he was referring to Buddy Lester and Norman Fell, who had been joined now by Henry Silva.

"I'll see you later, Eddie."

"Yeah, thanks again, Joey."

He went to join his *Ocean's 11* cohorts. I stood where I was for a few moments, because his comment about the "boys" — or my misunderstanding of it — had made me think of something.

Since Frank and Sam Giancana were friends, was the mob boss coming to the premier?

"Come in," Frank's man, George Jacobs, said. "Mr. Sinatra will be with you in a minute or two."

"Thank you."

He closed the door behind us and disappeared into the suite. Frank's suite was almost identical to Dean's, except that it seemed to me to be a little larger. I wondered if that was a matter of ego with him? He was the Leader, he had top billing in the movie, maybe he wanted to be sure he had the larger suite. I knew it didn't matter to Dino, but to my mind Dean was a little less insecure than Sinatra seemed to be.

I hadn't been invited to help myself to a drink, so I just walked over to the bar and sat on a stool to wait.

Frank came out about five minutes later and approached me with his hand out.

"I'm sorry, Eddie," he said. "I was on the phone with Ava."

"Ava Gardner?" I couldn't help myself from asking.

"That's right," he said. "Drink?" He went around behind the bar.

"Uh, sure, bourbon."

"Rocks?"

"Yeah."

"Ava and me," he said, preparing two drinks, "we may be divorced, but we're still connected, you know?"

"She's a beautiful woman," was all I could think to say.

"Oh, she's more than that, Eddie," he said, handing me my drink, "much more than that, but you're not here to talk about Ava, are you?"

He picked up his own drink and faced me. He was wearing gray slacks and a white button-down shirt, open at the collar. On his feet he wore loafers, but no socks.

"No, I'm not," I said. "I went to the Golden Nugget, checked out Mary Clarke's room. It looks like she started to unpack, but didn't get to finish."

He stopped with his glass almost to his mouth and eyed me over the rim.

"Didn't get to — you mean, somebody stopped her?"

"Something stopped her," I said. "Her toiletries were in the bathroom, but she didn't unpack her clothes, and she didn't sleep in the bed."

"Anyone see her?"

I nodded. "When she checked in, but not after that. She didn't make any long distance calls and they can't tell if she made any calls locally."

"I called her," Frank said. "I doubt she made any calls on her own."

"But you can't be sure."

"No," he said, "all I'm sure of is that she didn't call me."

"Frank," I said, "is Giancana comin' to town for the premier?"

"No, why?"

"I was just wondering."

"He would, but he'd be hassled."

"Is he sending anyone?"

"Yeah," Frank said, "he's sending one of his men, out of respect."

"You know the man?"

"Sure," he said, "but that's not important. You don't need to know that."

"I might at some point."

"If it comes to that I'll tell you who he is," Frank promised. "What are you doin' to find out where Mary is?"

"I'm doin' all I can, Frank," I said. "I promise. I've got eyes and ears all over town."

"Okay, Eddie, okay," Frank said, "I believe you. It's just . . . she's a sweet kid, you know?"

"I know, Frank," I said. Then, "well, I don't know, but I'll take your word for it."

"I hope you can find her before the opening tomorrow night."

"She wasn't going to go to that, was she?" I asked.

"No," he said, "we're not that stupid. We're keeping this very discreet. Besides, Juliet will be there." I gave him a look. He shrugged. "I couldn't talk her out of it."

He had a beautiful kid like Mary Clarke on a string, plus Juliet Prowse, and Ava Gardner was still in his life. How long would it be before I heard about him going out with Marilyn Monroe? I couldn't imagine what it must be like to be Frank Sinatra.

"Okay, Frank, I better get moving."

He walked me to the door with his hand on my back. When we got there I remembered something.

"Oh, here."

He looked at me while I pulled his photo out of my pocket and gave it to him. He unfolded it and stared.

"I don't know who's going to end up in that room," I said. "I didn't think you wanted anyone to find that, so I glommed it."

"Good thinkin', Eddie." He tried to smooth it out.

"You can give her another one when we

find her," I said.

"Yeah," he said, giving up, "you're right."

I left him there, holding the crumpled photo in his hands.

FIFTEEN

On the one hand, I was relieved that Sam Giancana was not coming to Vegas. On the other, he was sending a representative. Then it hit me. If I wanted to know about Giancana I had a source — Jerry. He worked for Sinatra, but that was because MoMo *told* him to work for Sinatra.

I wasn't sure how willing Jerry would be to talk about Giancana or any other mob boss, but the only way to find out was to ask.

By the time I got him away from the ponies Jerry was ahead fifteen hundred.

"Pancakes are on me tomorrow," he said, as we reentered the casino.

"How about drinks now?" I asked.

"You're on."

As we went into the lounge I was relieved to see that Bev had either left for the day or was on her break. We grabbed a table. A waitress named Lisa — cute, short, brunette

— brought us our drinks and caught Jerry's eye.

"Wow," he said, watching her sashay back to the bar.

"Want me to introduce you?"

He turned his head and stared at me with a deer-in-the-headlights expression.

"I wouldn't know what to say," he answered. "I like hookers. Ya don't have to talk ta them, ya know?"

Well, I couldn't argue with him on that.

"Whorin's legal out here, ain't it?"

"Sure is."

He thought a moment, but before he went too far astray thinking about whores I brought him back.

"Jerry, how well do you know Sam Giancana?"

"Mr. Giancana?" he looked surprised. "I know him, but he don't mix with the likes of me."

"Too low on the totem pole?"

"Too Jewish," Jerry said. "I work for one of the New York families."

"Not Giancana?"

"Not directly."

"I thought you met Frank through him."

He sipped his beer and said, "Kinda."

"What's kinda mean?"

"It means it came down from Mr. Giancana," he said, "but I never talked to him direct."

"Oh."

"Ya look disappointed," Jerry said.

"Not disappointed." I realized he thought I was disappointed in him. "No, I was just curious, that's all."

"Did you talk to Mr. S.?"

"Yeah, I did."

"So what're we doin' next?"

"Right now we're going to finish our drinks and —" I stopped when I saw the bartender waving at me, a phone receiver in his hand. "Excuse me a minute."

I walked over and Harry handed me the phone.

"Eddie, I've been tryin' to track you down all mornin'," Danny said.

"What's up?"

"Remember I asked you if you looked in the bathtub when you were at the Nugget?"

"Yeah, so?"

"You should've."

"Why?" I asked, with a cold feeling.

"Because there's a dead body in it."

I closed my eyes.

"Is it her?"

"No, it's some guy," he said, "probably dead since the night she got here."

"Jesus, how?"

94

"I didn't look real close, but I think he was clubbed to death. We got a lot of blood, here."

"I didn't see any blood in the room."

"It's all in the tub."

"How could that be?"

"Beats me, but it's not my job to figure it out."

"Where are you?"

"I'm in Dave Lewis' office. He's shittin' bricks here. We've got to call the cops, and we have to tell 'em somethin' about how we came to be lookin' for the girl and found a body." His tone became very apologetic. "I can't keep you out of it, ol' buddy, and even if I could I doubt that Dave could."

I put my hand to my forehead and looked over at big Jerry. We had a history of bodies and we had just added to it.

"Okay," I said, "okay, thanks for the heads up, Danny. I'm sorry I got you into this."

"Hey, all I've got to do is call the cops and tell 'em what I know," he said. "I've got the easy part. Good luck, buddy."

I handed the phone back to Harry. I had a few hours at least before the cops came looking for me. I had to use that time to get my story straight with Jerry, Jack Entratter, and with Frank.

Sixteen

I had to get to Frank in a hurry so we went right to his suite. I figured he'd still be there, since it wasn't long since we had talked. His man, George, answered the door and frowned at me.

"You don't have an appointment —"

"I need to talk to him right away," I said. "It's urgent."

"Well . . . will he know what it's about?"

"Oh, he'll know."

"Wait there, please."

He closed the door in our faces.

"Want me to get us in?" Jerry asked.

"How?"

"The old boot." He showed his size fourteen shoe.

"I don't think we'll have to do that, Jerry," I said. "On top of everything else we don't want to damage hotel property."

"I just meant puttin' my foot in the door next time he opens it."

"Oh, well, let's play it by ear."

When the door opened again it was Frank himself, not George.

"Come on in, Eddie," he said. "Hey, Jerry, how are you?"

"Good, Mr. S."

Frank closed the door and turned to face us, dressed as he had been before.

"What's goin' on, Eddie?"

"Plenty." I told him that a man's body had been found in Mary Clarke's room, in the bathtub.

"Who is he?"

"We don't know yet," I said, "but the police are sure to come looking for me."

"Why?"

"The house dick has to give them my name."

"We can't avoid that?"

"I doubt it."

"We can't . . . keep it from happening?"

A look passed between Frank and Jerry and I stepped between them.

"No, Frank," I said, "I think we're gonna have to deal with this."

"Whataya got in mind?"

"I'll talk to the cops and keep you out of it as long as I can," I said.

"What're you gonna tell them?"

"That I was looking for this girl for one of

97

my high rollers."

"You gonna get away with that?"

"Probably for a while," I said. "It'll give you time to come up with a story, get a lawyer . . . whatever you have to do."

Frank frowned and thought it over.

"I'm sorry, Frank," I said, "I don't think I can do anything else."

"It's okay," he said, waving his hand. "You do what you gotta do without getting' yourself jammed up."

He looked at Jerry.

"How much do you know?"

"Only what Dino told me, Mr S.," Jerry said. "I'm supposed to help Eddie."

"Well, watch his back," Frank said. "Where there's one dead body there might be more."

Neither one of us — Frank or me — said anything about the next one maybe being the girl.

"Frank, I've got to talk to Jack, too."

"Entratter?" he asked, just to make sure we were talking about the same person.

I nodded.

"I tell you what," he said. "I'll call him right now, tell him maybe I got his man into trouble again."

"Okay," I said, "that'll help. I'll go down there now. You'll probably be done by the time I get to his office."

"Go."

He turned to open the door, then turned back.

"Listen . . . you're still gonna look for her, aren't you? I mean, it's pretty obvious she's in trouble."

"Yeah," I said, "I'm still going to look for her."

He nodded, shook my hand and let us out.

Jerry was quiet until we got into the elevator.

"I was thinkin' —"

"Don't, Jerry."

"What?"

"You're not gonna strong-arm Dave Lewis."

"Why would I do that?" he asked. "Besides, your buddy Bardini is gonna give you up. So what good would it do for me to strong-arm the house dick?"

"Sorry, I thought that was the message going back and forth between you and Frank."

"It was," Jerry said, "but I wouldn't do that without checking with you first, Mr. G."

"I appreciate that, Jerry. So what were you gonna say, then?"

He seemed to have changed his mind, maybe because I'd insulted him.

He shrugged and said, "I was just thinkin' . . ."

SEVENTEEN

I knew detective Sam Hargrove of the Las Vegas Police. It had been him and his partner, a colored man named Smith, I'd dealt with the first time I'd found a body.

"Where's your partner?" I asked as he entered Jack Entratter's office.

"It's a bold new equal opportunity world," he said. "He got promoted. This is my partner, Detective Les Gorman."

Gorman blinked at me with watery blue eyes, brushed back a lock of snow white hair that had fallen over his forehead. He looked about a foot from retirement age.

By the time I'd gotten to Entratter's office earlier, he and Frank had, indeed, finished talking. He'd asked me to fill him in, then told me that when the cops came looking for me I should see them in his office.

"In fact," he'd said, "they'll probably come to me first, so I'll arrange it."

"How can you be so sure they'll come to

you first?"

He'd looked at me and said, "I'll arrange it."

True to his word when the detectives wanted me they called on him first. He'd told me to stay in the casino where he could find me, and told me to lose Jerry.

"We don't want him talkin' to the cops," he'd said. Jerry had been arrested last time, and Entratter had gotten him out. As it turned out Hargrove would remember him.

"Well, Eddie," Hargrove said, "it's been six months since you found a body."

"I didn't find this one."

"Oh, that's right," he said, "you didn't look in the bathtub . . . did you?"

"No, I didn't."

"You want to tell me what you were looking for?"

"Mary Clarke," I said. "Why else would I be in her room?"

"I don't know, you tell me."

Gorman stood off to one side, rocking back and forth, watching.

"Your new partner doesn't talk much."

"Don't change the subject."

"Just an observation."

"I talk when I've got something to say," Gorman responded.

"Which isn't now," Hargrove said, giving the man a pointed look. "Come on, Eddie, you've had enough time to think up a good story. Let's hear it."

"I don't have a story," I said. "I only have the truth."

"Well," Hargrove said, "that'll be different."

I didn't know if he was referring to me, or if it was just a general comment. I didn't ask.

Briefly, I told him that I had gone to the hotel looking for Mary Clarke because she had not been heard from since arriving in Las Vegas. I knew she had checked in, so I went to the house dick, Dave Lewis, and asked him to have a look.

"And he invited you up with him?"

"That's right."

"And neither one of you touched anything?"

I shrugged.

"I don't know. You mean because of fingerprints? I wasn't trying to hide the fact that I was there. Dave must've touched the doorknob so we could get in."

"Never mind," Hargrove said. "What'd you see when you were inside?"

I told him what Dave Lewis and I had found and didn't leave anything out. I didn't have to. He hadn't yet asked the question I was going to have to sidestep.

"And you never thought to look in the bathtub?" Hargrove asked when I was done.

"I didn't look under the bed, either, Detective," I said. "It just never occurred to me."

"Well, luckily it occurred to your buddy, Bardini. What was he doing there, by the way?"

"He was just helping me out."

"You hired him?"

I was about to say no when I noticed Jack Entratter nodding his head slightly.

"Yeah, that's right."

I didn't know if either of the detectives had caught my boss's head nod.

"To help you find the girl?"

"Right again."

I was tense, waiting for the big question.

Hargrove turned and looked at Jack Entratter, who was seated behind his desk. Jack gave him nothing, keeping his face still, but he asked a question of his own, giving me a break.

"Who's the dead guy, Detective?"

"We're still trying to i.d. him," Hargrove said. "He had nothing on him, not even a label on his jacket. I'd be grateful if somebody from here — you, Gianelli, whoever

— would come down to the morgue and have a look at him, maybe take a shot at identifying him."

"We can do that," Entratter said. "I'll have somebody from security come down. How was he killed?"

"Beaten to death with something," Hargrove said.

"I didn't see any blood in the room," I pointed out.

"Is that supposed to be helpful?" he asked.

I shrugged.

"Whoever the killer was put him in the tub first, then did him there."

"Was he carrying?" Entratter asked.

Hargrove looked at him.

"He was wearing a holster," he said. "It was empty. That was a good question."

Now Entratter shrugged. "It just came to me."

Hargrove nodded, then looked back at me.

"Okay, Eddie," he said, "why were you looking for this girl?"

I moved my shoulders uncomfortably.

"I was just helping out one of my high rollers."

"Married?"

"Of course."

"Bringing the girl in for a little slap and tickle?" he asked.

"Probably for more than that."

"Definitely more than that," Hargrove said. "I need a name."

I looked at Entratter.

"Detective, I'm sure you understand that we have to protect our whales." Jack used the universal casino word for high rollers.

"I'm investigating a murder here, Mr. Entratter," Hargrove reminded him.

"I can appreciate that." I was surprised at how educated Jack sounded when he was talking to the cops. But I guess that was his strength as a casino general manager, the ability to adapt.

"This girl's family has a right to know what's going on," Hargrove said.

"The girl isn't the one who's dead," Jack Entratter reminded him.

"Well then . . . the dead man's family has a right."

"And you don't know who his family is, yet," Entratter said. "Tell you what I'll do. Let Eddie talk to our whale and we'll see if we can't get him to come to you on his own."

"And if he doesn't?"

Entratter shrugged his wide shoulders.

"Then I suppose we won't have any choice but to cooperate."

Hargrove studied Entratter for a few moments, then looked at me again.

"I'm going to hold you to your word," he said to Jack while still looking at me.

"That's fine, Detective."

Hargrove pointed a finger at me.

"You skated six months ago, but I knew you were dirty then," he said. "So that leads me to believe you're dirty this time, too."

"What am I supposed to say to that?"

"Nothing," he said. "Nothing at all. But when I want you to talk, you will. I promise you that."

I didn't know what to say to that, either, so I kept quiet.

"Come on, Les."

Hargrove headed for the door and his partner, Gorman, followed him out without a word. That left me and Entratter alone.

"Take a seat."

I sat across from him.

"I'm not givin' them Frank, Eddie."

"How can you avoid it?"

"You're gonna fix this for me," he said. "You and your buddies — Jerry and your P.I. friend."

"How, Jack?"

"Find the girl."

"And if she's dead?"

"Find the killer."

"That's asking a lot."

107

He leaned all the way back in his chair and regarded me for a moment, his hands folded in front of him. I didn't like how calm he was.

"How about if your job depended on it."

"What?" I shot forward in my chair. "You can't be serious, Jack."

"Put yourself in my place, kid," he said, reasonably. "Who would you rather lose, a pit boss named Eddie G.? Or Frank Sinatra?"

"Damn it, Jack," I said, sitting back in my chair miserably, "when you put it that way . . ."

EIGHTEEN

I found Jerry on the casino floor, watching a high stakes blackjack table near my pit. There were three players at the table and I knew them all as regulars. Two were men, one a woman. She was the best player of the three.

"That old guy with the gray hair," Jerry said, "he wins a lot."

"He has amazing luck."

"And the broad with the big tits?"

"She plays well, but has no luck."

"What's that mean?"

"She does everything right, plays by the rules, and still manages to just about break even."

"There's rules?"

"Unwritten rules," I said.

"And the guy?"

"He takes chances, goes against the rules, but his luck holds and he makes money."

"And the third guy?"

"He plays every hand," I said. "Some he wins, some he doesn't. Usually goes home a loser."

"You know all of 'em?"

"Well," I said. "They're always here."

"You ever tap that broad?"

"Jerry . . ."

"I'm just wonderin' about them tits," the big man said.

"She's married, has three kids and one grandchild."

His eyes went wide.

"That broad's a grandma?"

"A damned good-looking one," I said. "She comes here to play cards, not to play."

"Too bad," he said. "So, what happened upstairs with the cops?"

"You remember Detective Hargrove from last year? Took you in?"

"I remember."

"He's got this case."

"Does he know about me?"

"No yet, but he's after my ass."

"Is Mr. Entratter gonna cover it?"

"Mr. Entratter is gonna hang my ass out to dry if it means keepin' Frank clean."

He frowned.

He took his eyes off grandma's chest. "That ain't right."

"Maybe not," I said, "but it's how the

110

game is played out here. Come on."

"Where to?"

"I've got to talk to both Dave Lewis and Danny, again."

"We takin' the Caddy?" he asked, keeping up with me easily even though he was taking one stride to my two.

"Yep," I said. I took out the keys and tossed them in the air. He caught them.

First we stopped in the lobby so I could use a pay phone. There were two lines of people at the front desk, one checking in and one checking out. The check-out line was shorter. The Sands was one of the hottest spots on the strip, especially when one of the Rat Pack was performing there.

I called Danny to see if he was in. He was and he agreed to meet us at the Golden Nugget, in Dave Lewis' office.

When we got there I called Dave from the lobby and he told us to come ahead. Danny was already seated in a chair in front of Dave's desk when we arrived.

"I'm sorry I got you guys into this," I started.

"Hey," Dave said with a shrug, "we had to find that body some time."

"Like I said before," Danny added, "your ass is the one on the line."

111

"You don't know the half of it."

I told them both what Entratter had told me.

"It ain't fair," Jerry said, echoing his original sentiment.

"No, it ain't," Danny said, "but it doesn't surprise me."

"Me, neither. I'd get the boot, too, if it meant keeping Tony Bennett here."

"Stuff that's done in New York is a lot more honest," Jerry said. "If somebody's ass is on the line it's for a good reason."

"And then you break it," Dave Lewis said.

Jerry gave him a hard look.

"Yeah," he said, "that's my job, and I do it real good."

"I'll bet you do," Dave said. I didn't know why he was poking at Jerry, but I didn't want him to do it anymore.

"Okay, forget all that," I said. "Dave, when you talked to the cops did you tell them everything?"

"Everything I knew."

"What about Jerry?' I asked. "Did you tell them about Jerry?"

Dave looked at the big man, smiled and asked, "Who's Jerry?"

The big guy took a step forward, as if insulted but I put my arm out to stop him.

"He left you out of it," I said.

"He did?"

I nodded, and he took a step back.

"Danny?"

"I never mentioned the big guy," Danny said.

"I told the cops I hired you."

"Okay, I'll go along with that story."

"Does that mean you can keep stuff from them?"

Danny shook his head. "I'm a P.I., not a lawyer. You want legal confidentiality you'll have to hire a lawyer, and then I can work for him. What are you keeping from them, anyway?"

"The name of the man who asked me to look for the girl."

"Oh."

"Who is it?" Dave asked.

"You don't need ta know," Jerry told him.

"Oh yeah? Well, maybe I suddenly remembered I should tell the cops about you."

"Dave," I said, "come on . . ."

"Ah, forget it," he said. "You're right, I don't need to know. Maybe you guys should just take the rest of this — whatever it is you're doin' — outside."

"You're right, Dave," I said. "Thanks for your help, so far."

"Yeah, yeah." He sat back in his chair and looked the other way. His feelings were probably hurt.

"One more thing," I said, at the door.

"What?"

"Is the room still sealed? The girl's room?"

"It's a fucking crime scene," he said. "Yeah, it's sealed."

"Are the girl's belonging inside?"

"No, the cops took 'em."

"Thanks, Dave," I said. "I won't bother you with this anymore."

NINETEEN

I found Danny and Jerry on the casino floor. The big guy was looking around like a kid at Disneyland.

"This place is huge," he said.

"The Nugget is special," Danny said.

From where we stood we could hear nickels hitting the coin trays of the slots, shooters rattling the bones in their hands before rolling, blackjack dealers calling out the buy-ins at their tables — "Changing a hundred!" — to their pit bosses. Also, I could pick out the distinctive sound of the little white ball bouncing around on the roulette wheel before it came to a stop on a number, and the moans of losers drowning out the elated cries of the winner — all of them everyday sounds to me.

"What's next?" Jerry asked.

Danny looked at me.

"Can you get your high roller to voluntarily talk to the police?"

"I don't know," I said. "I could ask him, but that would put me in Dutch with Entratter."

"Your ass is on the line, Eddie, with more than just your boss," Danny said. "Don't forget that."

"I won't. Did you get a chance to talk to the doormen, valets and drivers to see if any of them saw the girl?"

"Didn't get the chance," Danny said. "Finding a body kinda put a crimp in my plans. I'll get on it now. What about you and Jerry?"

I scratched my head.

"I'm not sure, Danny."

"What about the body?" Jerry asked.

We both looked at him.

"What?" I asked.

"We could go to the morgue and take a look," Jerry said. "If he's a made guy I might know who he is."

"Danny? You didn't recognize him, did you?"

"If he's mobbed up he ain't local," Danny said, shaking his head. "If he's imported, maybe the big guy has a point. He might know him."

"The cops did ask Entratter to send someone to the morgue." I looked at Jerry. "If you go, Hargrove might recognize you while you're lookin' at the body. That okay with you?"

Jerry shrugged.

"What can he do to me? I ain't done nothin'."

"He could try to make your life miserable."

Jerry laughed shortly. "Lots of people already beat him to it."

"I'll have to call Jack, see if he sent somebody down there already."

"Nah," Danny said, "just go and tell the attendant you're there to take a look. He won't care. That way, you might miss bein' seen by Hargrove."

I slapped Jerry on the back.

"That's what we're gonna do," I said. "If you know the guy maybe that'll tell us something."

"Maybe," Jerry said. He still had my Caddy keys in his pocket and jingled them.

"Let's check in later and compare notes," Danny said, as we all walked to the door. "And think about that lawyer."

"I'll talk to Jack," I said. "The Sands has lawyers up the ass."

"All you need is one," he said.

TWENTY

I shivered as we walked out of the elevator into the hospital basement.

"Never been down to a morgue before?" Jerry asked.

"No."

"Scared?"

"No," I said. "It's just . . . givin' me the creeps. And it's cold."

"That's so the stiffs don't stink —"

"I know that, Jerry."

After a few more steps he muttered, "Sorry."

"Forget it," I said. "I'm . . . just forget it."

When we got to the reception desk I told them I had been sent there by the Sands hotel to try to identify a body.

"Both of you?" the attendant asked.

"That's right," I said. "My boss figured one of us might know him."

"Hey," the man said, "no skin off my nose. I just need ya both to sign in."

He pushed a clipboard toward us, then turned his back. I thought he was kind of young to have that big of a bald spot on the crown of his head.

I leaned over and whispered, "Don't give your real name."

Jerry nodded and wrote, "Mike Mazurki."

I took the pen and signed my name.

"We're ready," I said.

The attendant looked at the clipboard, then glanced quickly at Jerry.

"Hey, really nice to meet ya," he said, grabbing Jerry's hand. "I enjoy your work."

"Thanks," Jerry said.

"Workin' for the Sands now?"

"Yeah."

"Well, come this way," he said. "He's on a slab waitin' for ya."

We followed him through double swinging doors and into a room that was even colder than outside. Without any warning he whipped a sheet off the body, which was on a slab, naked.

"Take your time," he said. "I'll be outside."

Jerry walked up to the body and looked down at him. He took his time, studied the face closely, then stepped back next to me.

"I don't know the stiff."

"Then he's not imported talent?" I asked.

119

"Not from New York," Jerry said, " 'cause if he was I'd know 'im."

"Great," I said, "that only leaves forty-nine other states."

"You gonna take a look?"

"What?"

"You know," he said, "see if you know the guy?"

"Hey, if Danny didn't know him, I'm not gonna know him," I reasoned.

Jerry gave me a disappointed look, then said, "Suit yerself."

"Wait," I said, as he started for the door. "I didn't say I wouldn't look. All I said was I probably wouldn't know him."

I stepped forward, steeled myself and took a look at the dead guy's face. The rest of his body was unmarked — obviously, no autopsy had been done yet — but his head was severely damaged. However, his face was also unmarked, and as I stared down at him I realized I did know him.

"Christ," I said.

"What?"

I turned to Jerry. "Let's get out of here."

TWENTY-ONE

"What happened in there?" Jerry asked when we had the car on the road again.

"I knew that guy."

"Oh. Was he a friend of yours?"

"No, no," I said. "I mean, I knew him, but I didn't really know him. Understand?"

"Perfectly."

"You do?"

"Sure," he said, with a shrug. "You know him, but you don't know his name."

"Exactly!"

"So where do you know him from?"

"I've seen him," I said, "but I can't remember where, or when."

"That won't be real helpful to the cops."

"Don't I know it," I said. "I'm gonna have to rack my brain to try and figure this one out."

"Maybe I can help."

"How?"

"I dunno. You could just talk ta me, maybe

somethin' will click."

"Like a sounding board?"

"I don't know what that is," Jerry said, "but yeah, if it'll work."

"Maybe it was at the casino."

"Like at the tables?" he asked. "Like those other players that you see every day?"

"Not a regular." I shook my head. "I'd know him if he was a regular."

"Maybe he was just passin' through."

"Or hanging around . . . waiting."

"What for?"

"That's the question."

"Maybe he was watchin' you."

"Me?" I didn't like the sound of that. "Why would he do that?"

"Hopin' you'd lead him to the girl."

"But she was already missing."

"Maybe he was supposed to find 'er and kill 'er," he suggested.

"But why?" I asked. "And does it have anything to do with Frank?"

Jerry shrugged.

"I've got to figure this out," I said, "and when I do I'll have to go to the cops."

"They won't appreciate it," Jerry warned.

"Probably not," I agreed, thinking of Detective Hargrove.

"Hey, if that guy was in Vegas to kill the

girl," Jerry said, "then that contract is still open."

"Contract? On a young girl?"

"That kinda stuff don't care nothin' about age," Jerry replied. "If she got on somebody's wrong side . . ."

"The poor kid. She's probably out there somewhere, scared shitless."

"Or," Jerry said, "maybe she's dead."

"What do you mean? If he was a hit man and he ended up dead —"

"Sometimes those guys travel in pairs," he said, "so if there's another one out there you're racin' him to the girl."

"Oh, great, so now I'm chasing after a hit man."

Jerry was silent, but it felt to me like he had something to say.

"What?"

He looked at me.

"Could be he's chasing after you."

TWENTY-TWO

We went back to the Sands. I stopped bouncing things off of Jerry after he said the hit man might be chasing me. I didn't want to hear any more. I didn't need to be thinking about some guy whose business was killing being on my trail. All I was supposed to do was find a girl who had gotten lost — not dead.

Jerry left his extra bag in my car, in case we went back home that night. After my conversation with him, I wasn't sure that was such a good idea. I had access to a room at the Sands anytime I wanted it, and that was my thought.

"What do we do now?" he asked as we entered through a back door.

"I want to see if Jack sent anyone over to the morgue to view the body," I said. "If he did maybe that person recognized him."

"The guy at the morgue didn't say nothin' about nobody bein' there already."

124

"Maybe they got there after we left," I said. "If not, I'll ask Jack to send somebody from security, like he said he would."

The area above the ceiling over the casino floor was a maze of catwalks and one-way mirrors the casino used to observe the table games, looking for cheaters. I wondered if somebody up there would recognize this guy.

In any case, Entratter should be made aware that I knew the guy, possibly from the casino.

"Can I watch some more blackjack while you talk to him?" Jerry asked.

"Jerry," I said, "you can watch all the blackjack you want."

I left Jerry at one of my tables and told the guy on the pit to keep an eye on him. Then I went to Entratter's office to tell him the news.

"First of all," he asked, "what the hell were you doin' down there? Didn't I say I was gonna send somebody?"

"I just wanted to see if I knew the guy, for my own benefit. Also, I thought Jerry might know him."

"What made you think that?"

"Somebody killed the guy. He must've gone there with bad intentions."

"So it was you who recognized him, and not the torpedo?"

"Right."

"Okay," he said, "I'll send somebody."

"I also want to talk to whoever was the eye in the sky yesterday," I said, "see if maybe they saw something, or knew the guy."

"You go upstairs and I'll call ahead," he said. "Larry'll tell you whatever you want."

Larry Bigbee was second-in-command in Security. He and I had played poker a time or two in some private games.

"Okay, Jack, thanks."

"Glad to help."

Sure you are, I thought as I left. You hang my ass out to dry and you're only too happy to help me try to save it, as long as you don't have to get too hands-on about it.

Larry didn't know the guy I was talking about, but he surprised me with something.

"I've been takin' a camera up there with me."

"What for?"

He shrugged.

"Just to take some pictures, maybe start a file on blackjack players. I'm thinkin' this may be somethin' I want to start up when I make it to the number one spot."

Larry was always talking about innovations he'd like to make when he got to be head of Security. This one sounded good to me.

"Can you show me some of the film you shot?"

"Sure thing."

He pulled out the black-and-white shots he'd taken over the last few days and spread them out on his desk.

"That's him."

Larry said, "I'll make you a copy of this photo."

"Is he in any others?"

We both went through them again, but there was only one shot of the guy. He was playing blackjack at a low-limit table. There was a time and date written on the bottom of the photo.

"I'll talk to Gabe Daniels," Larry promised. "He was on the catwalk during that shift, also. Maybe he spotted your guy."

"Thanks, Larry."

"Where should I send the copy of the photo?"

"Send it to Jack's girl. I'll pick it up from her later this evening."

"You got it."

We shook hands and I left.

■ ■ ■ ■

"What happened?" Jerry asked.

"We've got a photo of him," I said. "He was sitting at one of my tables." I pointed. "That one." There were two little old ladies and a guy in a loud shirt sitting there now.

"Want me to check out the guy?"

"No," I said. "I know him. He comes in all the time."

"And the old ladies?"

"Probably tourists."

"Want me to check them out?"

"No, Jerry," I said. "Leave the little old ladies alone."

"I'm hungry."

"Let's hit the buffet."

I left Jerry at the buffet and used a house phone to let Jack's girl know she'd be getting a photo for me. She told me that if I didn't come for it by the end of her work day she'd leave it in her unlocked desk drawer. I thanked her and joined Jerry at the buffet. He had left me barely enough room at the table for my one plate.

"You can go back, you know," I said.

"I know," he replied. "This is just my first course."

"You've got enough fried chicken there to feed an army."

"I grew up poor," he said. "If you didn't grab what you wanted right away, it wasn't there no more."

"Yeah, well," I said, "I didn't grow up poor, but it was pretty much that way in my family, too."

Poor, middle class, there was still a food budget in the house. Jerry was so busy eating he had no room for conversation, which was okay by me. I had some serious thinking to do.

Twenty-Three

Did I want to be involved with a hit man?
No. Did I want to disappoint Frank Sinatra? No. Did I want that poor girl to end up
dead if she wasn't already? No. Did I want
to back out of this whole business? Hell,
yeah. But would I?

"Ain't you goin' back?" Jerry asked after
his second assault at the buffet.

"No," I said. "I had enough."

"I'm goin' for dessert." He stood up.
"Want somethin'?"

"Will you be able to carry it back for me?"
I asked.

He glowered down at me. "My mama
used ta say nobody likes a wisenheimer."

"Okay, bring me back a piece of cherry
pie, then."

As I watched Jerry walk to the dessert station I recalled hearing that it was Herb Mc-
Donald — a well-known promoter in Vegas
— who was credited with inventing the

concept of the buffet almost fifteen years ago at the El Rancho Vegas, the very first of the Vegas Casinos — even predating Bugsy's Flamingo. The story goes Herb was hungry one night and asked the kitchen to bring some cold meats, cheeses and bread out to the bar. Some gamblers came walking by, said they were hungry and the buffet was born. The original was called the "Midnight Chuckwagon" and the cost was $1.25.

The buffet's popularity had been growing by leaps and bounds ever since. I wondered how many Jerry Epsteins it would take to run them out of business?

Jerry came back with my cherry pie and several slices of cakes and pies for himself, all balanced up and down his arms.

"Used ta wait tables when I was a kid," he said, sitting down.

"Very impressive."

He got us some coffee and we ate our desserts. Despite the amount of food he devoured, Jerry had good table manners. He was full of surprises, this mountain of a man. He could be very brutal — I'd seen it firsthand — and yet he was well-mannered most of the time. I was willing to bet he had been raised alone by his mother.

I decided not to ask, though.

We got to Jack's Entratter's office late. True to her word, his girl had left the photo in the middle drawer of her desk, the only one that was unlocked. Jerry checked them all.

"Old habit," he said with an apologetic shrug. "Thought she might have some gum."

I showed him the photo by the light of the green-shaded desk lamp.

"I still don't know him."

"Damn it, neither do I, but there he is in black and white."

"Maybe that's the only time you ever saw him," Jerry suggested. "No reason why you should remember. He don't look like much."

"His face stuck in my mind for some reason." I sat down in the desk chair.

"Did you talk to him?"

I stared at the photo, trying to remember.

"I don't think so."

"Did you have to do somethin'?" he asked. "Okay some money or somethin'?"

"He's not sitting at a high limit table," I said. "I doubt it."

"Maybe he talked to you, asked a question?"

"Wait a minute . . ." Suddenly, I could see his face in front of me, but what was he saying?

"So he did ask you a —"

"Shh, wait." I almost had it. "It's gone."

"Sorry."

"It's not your fault, Jerry," I said. "It's my damn memory."

I got up.

"Let's go," I said. "We're gonna stay in the hotel tonight."

"Will the Caddy be safe in the parking lot?" Jerry asked as we left the office.

"I don't know, but we'll be safe."

"You don't have to worry about nothin', Mr. G.," he said, putting his big arm around my shoulder. "I ain't gonna let nothin' happen to ya."

"I'm touched, Jerry."

"Mr. S. would have my ass."

"It's nice to know you care. . . ."

133

TWENTY-FOUR

Danny called me that night in my room at the Sands. He figured if I wasn't at home that was where I'd be.

"I talked with the valets," he said, "parking lot attendants, doormen . . . showed her photo. Nobody saw her leave."

"What do you make of that?" I asked.

"I figure she's in Vegas for the first time; if she left the hotel on her own it would've been by the front door."

"So if she went out the back," I finished, "somebody took her that way?"

"That's my guess."

I told him what Jerry had told me about the possibility of two hit men.

"Makes sense," he said, "but I don't think a second guy has her."

"Why not?"

"Why take 'er?" he asked. "Why not just kill her in her room?"

"And who killed the one at the morgue?"

"Maybe she did," Danny said. "Maybe she got lucky."

"And then she ran? And somebody helped her?"

"A good-lookin' blonde?" he asked. "How hard would it be for her to get some help?"

"From a guy who works at the Nugget."

"I'll get on that tomorrow," he said. "Maybe the guy won't show up for work — if there is a guy."

"Thanks, Danny."

"What are you gonna do?"

"Try and stay out of the line of fire of a hit man, I guess."

"Stand behind Jerry," he suggested. "That should do it."

I hung up, thought about turning on the TV, but decided against it. I sat on the bed with my shoes off. I'd called for room service a few minutes earlier because I wanted a pot of coffee. When the knock came at the door, I was proud of the Sands for taking such good care of its guests. But when I opened the door, a man stuck a gun in my face and I cursed myself for being careless.

"Inside," he said.

"T-thought you were room service."

"You ain't gonna get to eat tonight."

He stepped inside and closed the door.

135

He was tall, almost gangly, about my age, and he had a Brooklyn accent.

"I-it was just coffee."

"Sit on the bed."

I did.

"On your hands."

Crap. I did it. We were in a standard-sized room. I got it on a comp, but I didn't rate a suite. That meant he was too damn close to me with that gun for comfort.

"Where is she?"

"Where's who?"

"Don't get cute with me, pit boss," he snarled. "I ain't in the mood. My partner's dead and my target is on the run. I ain't got the time."

"Your target?"

"Don't act stupid," he said. "You're clued in, you know the score."

"I don't," I said, "really. The score's a mystery to me." I was babbling, I knew I was, but I was looking down the barrel of a gun. That was not an everyday occurrence for me.

"You work for Entratter," the man said. "That means you're on the inside."

"I work for the Sands," I said. "I'm just a pit boss."

"Then why are you lookin' for the girl?"

"I was just doing somebody a favor."

136

"Who?"

"One of my high rollers."

He poked the air with his gun and said, "Who, damn it?"

Frank's name was on the tip of my tongue but I decided I'd be damned if I'd give it to this bum.

"Who hired you to kill her?" I asked, instead. "What's she done to anybody that'd get her killed?"

"I don't ask those kinds of questions," he said. "I just do my job."

"Well, if the girl's on the loose and your partner's dead," I said, "you suck at it."

His hand tightened on the butt of his automatic and just when I thought I'd gone too far there was a knock on the door.

"That'd be real room service," I said.

"Don't answer."

"I have to. I work here, they know I'm here. They'll wonder what —"

"Tell 'em to leave it outside the door."

"They don't do that here," I said. I was playing for time. What good was the room service waiter going to do me? And I didn't want to get him killed, too.

"Okay," he said, "okay, get the door, but don't say nothin'. I'll kill the both of you."

I got up off the bed. He stepped aside to let me approach the door.

137

"Any funny stuff and you're both dead," he repeated his threat. "Remember."

I still had no idea what I was going to do as I opened the door, but it didn't matter. Jerry's left hand shot out, grabbed me and pulled me into the hall. At the same time he fired the .45 he held in his right. It bucked once, made a deafening sound in the hall, and then went quiet.

"You okay, Mr. G.?" he asked.

I peered into the room, saw the hit man flat on his back on the bed, blood seeping from his chest. His gun was on the floor.

"I am now," I said. "How'd you know?"

He smiled at me.

"I tol' you I wouldn't let nothin' happen to you," he said. "I was on watch down the hall."

He stepped into the room, checked the guy to see if he was dead, then kicked the hit man's gun under the bed.

"Know him?" I asked.

"Uh-uh," he said. "I never saw him before. What about you?"

"Nope."

"Did he say anythin' helpful?"

"Actually he did," I said, "but right now we've got to come up with a story for the cops."

"Why?"

"So you don't get into trouble."

"Why should I get into trouble?" he asked. "I'm licensed to carry my gun, and I saved your life. You can tell them everythin' he said."

"You mean . . . you don't care if I call the cops?" I asked.

"Mr. G.," he said, as if scolding me, "you gotta call the cops. It's your duty as a good citizen."

I heard doors opening in the halls, guests no doubt peering out to find out what was going on.

"Okay, Jerry," I said. "Why don't you close the door and I'll make the call."

But I had to call Jack Entratter first. I didn't know who this was going to piss off more, him or Detective Hargrove.

TWENTY-FIVE

It was a toss-up.

It only took an hour for the room to fill up with cops. Some were in uniform, some in plain clothes. They were talking to guests in the hall, taking pictures of the dead body, fishing the gun out from under the bed, bagging both it and Jerry's gun and, oh yeah, putting Jerry Epstein in cuffs for saving my life.

"Is that really necessary?" I demanded.

Hargrove put his hand on my chest and said, "You're lucky you're not in cuffs, Eddie."

"For what?" Jack Entratter asked, entering at that moment. "For almost getting killed?"

"We got a dead man here, Mr. Entratter," Hargrove said. "If Eddie is right and he's the partner of the guy we got on a slab down at the morgue, then they're both hitters from New York."

"Not New York," Jerry said, calmly. "If

they was from New York I'd know 'em."

"Shut up," Hargrove said. "I'm not talking to you. Not yet, anyway." He looked at the uniformed cop who had put his cuffs on Jerry. "Take him downtown, put him in a holding room."

"Hey," I said, "all he did was —"

I was cut off by both my boss and Hargrove, who then got into a shouting match of their own. Jerry gave me a little shrug as the cop led him out of the room. The body was still on the bed. It had stopped bleeding when the heart stopped beating, but there was still a bloody Sands bed quilt that was going to have to go.

I have to say I admired Hargrove. I thought he had always been a little intimidated by Entratter, but as their voices grew louder he gave as good as he got.

"I'm conducting an inquiry here, sir," Hargrove said, polite to the end. "If you interfere I'll have you put in cuffs, as well."

Entratter rocked back on his heels, and then he laughed shortly.

"You'd do that, wouldn't you, you little pissant?" he demanded.

"Try me."

Entratter wasn't laughing then. His face turned so red he looked even more like he was about to burst than usual.

"Jack, I've got it," I said to him, then I turned to Hargrove. "Look, your hitter, here, came bursting into my room and would've killed me if it wasn't for Jerry."

"The hitter's name is Frank Capistrello. His partner on the slab is Joey Favazza. They're cheap labor, freelancers trying to work themselves into one of the families."

"So you're sayin' you don't know who they work for?" Entratter demanded.

"That's right," Hargrove said, "we don't. Maybe we could have gotten something out of Frankie, here, if your torpedo hadn't killed him."

"He's not my torpedo —" Entratter said.

"He doesn't like being called that," I said. They both looked at me.

"What?" Hargrove asked.

"Jerry," I said, "he doesn't like being called that."

"Oh, Jesus . . ." Entratter said. Throwing his hands into the air.

"Well, whatever he likes to be called," Hargrove said, "he fixed it so this guy can't tell us anything."

"If not for Jerry," I argued, "I wouldn't be here telling you anything."

"You're *not* telling me anything, are you?"

"I'm tellin' you what I know!"

It got quiet all of a sudden. We looked

142

around and saw that everyone in the room was staring at us.

"What?" Hargrove demanded.

"Uh," his partner, Gorman said, "the medical examiner wants to take the body."

"Then tell him to take it, damn it." He glared around the room. "Everybody get to work!"

He turned to give me a glare of my own.

"What did he want?"

"All he had time to do was ask me where she is."

"Where who — the girl? He was asking about her?"

"That's right."

"And what did you tell him?"

"The truth. I don't know where she is."

"But you're looking, right?"

"I've got some feelers out."

"Because of your high roller, right?"

I nodded.

Hargrove looked at Entratter then. Who had nothing to say. The detective apparently had not yet decided to push for the name.

"How did Jerry know you were in trouble?"

"He said he was watching my room."

"So he expected something like this?"

"All he said was that he wouldn't let anything happen to me."

"So he could've stopped this guy before he got into your room?"

"You'll have to ask him that."

He pointed at me with his right index finger.

"I should put you in cuffs, too, and take you down for questioning."

"For what? Almost getting killed?" I demanded. "And you can ask me all the questions you want. I can't tell you any more than I have. I don't know this guy, never saw him before. Or his partner."

Well, that wasn't true, and if he bothered to search my clothes — my jacket — he'd find the photo of Joey Favazza in my pocket. But I opened my mouth and the lie came tumbling out.

"I'm gonna let you off the hook, Eddie," Hargrove said. "I'll be pretty busy questioning your buddy, anyway."

"I'll have a lawyer down there in twenty mimutes," Entratter said.

"I wouldn't expect anything less."

"Come on, Eddie," Jack said. "Let's get you another room."

I went to get my jacket, with the Favazza photo in it, and Hargrove said, "Don't disturb any evidence."

"I just want my jacket."

I waited, all my muscles tense while I tried

144

to look relaxed. I wanted to get that photo out of the room.

"Take it," he said, with a pissed-off wave.

I grabbed it and followed Jack into the hall.

"Jack, I —"

"Shut up!"

We walked to the elevators and after we'd stepped into one he asked, "What the hell happened?"

"Exactly what I told Hargrove," I said. "I was expecting room service and the guy stuck a gun in my face when I opened the door."

"If Jerry was watching your room," he demanded, "why didn't he stop the guy outside, like Hargrove asked?"

"And like I told Hargrove, I don't know," I said. "You are gonna get that lawyer down there, aren't you?"

"I should leave him there," he said. "The guy comes to Vegas twice and kills somebody both times."

"And both times to save my life."

"Yeah, yeah," he said. "Here." He handed me a key.

"A suite?"

"Enjoy," he said, "and use the peep hole if you order room service again."

"Believe me," I said, "I will."

TWENTY-SIX

I didn't order room service again because now I had a suite. Not as large as the ones Frank and Dean had, but still I had a bar and a well-stocked refrigerator. I had a few belts of good bourbon and then went to the window to look over the city. I could almost feel the heat of the neon bulbs. It soothed me. I had almost stopped shaking. A close call like that every six months was about all I could stand.

I got myself another drink and took it with me to the plush sofa. I didn't know I had fallen asleep until the phone rang and woke me. I fumbled for it, knocking over my empty glass.

"Huh? Hello?"

"Hey, Mr. G."

"Jerry? Where are you?"

"In my room," he said. "I just got back. Mr. Entratter brung me a lawyer and he got me sprung."

"Clean?"

"Naw," Jerry said, "I gotta go to court, for sure. Can't leave town for a while."

"Good for me," I said. "Listen, Jerry, I'm sorry you had to kill that guy."

"Hey, no sweat, Mr. G.," he said. "It's what I do, remember?"

"Yeah, well, maybe I just don't like you havin' to do it for me."

"You want me to come up to your room?"

"No," I said, "get some sleep. Meet me downstairs in the coffee shop at nine o'clock for breakfast. I don't think you've had the pancakes there yet. I owe you a big stack."

"Sounds good. I gotta go take a shower, get the cop stink offa me."

"Hey, Jerry."

"Yeah?'

"Did they ask you why you didn't stop that goon out in the hall?"

"Yeah, they did."

I waited, then asked, "Well . . . what did you tell them?"

I could hear his big shoulders shrug over the phone.

"I didn't think of it."

In the morning, before meeting Jerry for breakfast, I called Danny Bardini at home.

"This better be good," he groaned into

147

the phone when I told him it was me. "I was plannin' on sleepin' another hour."

I told him about the excitement the night before, and that woke him up.

"Man, that Jerry's your guardian angel, Eddie."

"You said it. Look, I don't know if this is gonna make the cops come lookin' for you again, but you might be getting a visit from Hargrove."

"No problem," he said, through a yawn. "I can handle him."

"Okay," I said. "See what you can do at the Nugget today, will you? We're on kind of a tight deadline here."

"I gotcha. I think I'm pretty much lookin' for a guy young enough to be impressed by a babe with blond hair and big tits."

"A young guy? How about any guy?"

"Ah, I'm not so sure an older guy would want to try to play hero, you know? But I could be wrong. I'll let you know what happens."

"Okay, thanks."

"Look, one thing."

"What's that?"

"We got two dead mechanics now."

"Not very good ones," I replied, "from what I've been told."

"Yeah, well, whoever sent them may send

148

some good ones, next time."

"Next time?"

"Eddie," he said, "if there's one thing I've learned in this business, it's that there's always a next time."

TWENTY-SEVEN

The way Jerry packed away the pancakes I owed him I was glad I hadn't owed him money.

"So did they tell you the names of the two guys?" I asked.

"Yeah," he said, with his mouth full. "Capistrello and Favazza."

"You ever hear of them in New York?"

He finished chewing and looked at me.

"Mr. G., I mostly hang out with made guys in New York," he said. "Guys who are in crews. They wouldn't even spit on those bums."

"So who would send those guys out here from New York?" I asked.

He shrugged and said, "Somebody without the connections to get better talent, or somebody who didn't want to use somebody inside. But I think a better question is who'd wanna whack some sweet kid?"

I studied him across the table, wondering

150

if he knew that the sweet kid was not only Frank Sinatra's girl, but MoMo Giancana's, as well?

"Jerry, you don't know this girl, do you?" I asked.

"I never seen her," he said, "and I only know her name 'cause the cops told me."

I remembered that Jerry had never seen the photo Frank had given me. I also remembered I hadn't gotten it back from Danny.

"She's a blonde, a real babe," I said. "Pale skin, knockers, the works."

"Like Marilyn?" he asked.

"Yes," I said, "like Marilyn."

"Don't make sense somebody would wanna put a dish like that down," he said. "Unless . . ."

"Unless what?"

"She's been sleepin' with the wrong guy."

"I think we both know who she's been sleeping with, Jerry."

"You mean Mr. S.," he said. "I don't talk about his business."

"I mean MoMo," I said, watching his face. "She's also sleepin' with Giancana."

Jerry hunched his shoulders.

"You ain't supposed ta talk about Mr. Giancana, Eddie."

"Maybe you're not supposed to talk about

151

him, but I can. See, I'm wondering if I'm caught between Frank and MoMo, here."

"You think Mr. Giancana sent those two to kill the broad because she's been sleepin' with Mr. S.?"

"Well, he wouldn't hit Frank would he?"

"Not over a broad," he said, without missing a beat.

"So what do you think, Jerry?"

Jerry sopped up some syrup with the last forkful of pancakes.

"Why you askin' me?"

"Because you're smarter than anybody gives you credit for," I said.

He looked at me.

"Ain't nobody ever said that to me before."

"Come on, Jerry," I said. "Give me your take on this."

He ate the last forkful and then put the utensil down. He wiped his mouth with a napkin before he spoke.

"I don't think Mr. Giancana would send no-talent bums like them to do a job," he said. "He just wouldn't do it. If he really wanted her dead he's got pros who can do it with no problem."

"What if MoMo — Mr. Giancana — didn't want it to look like him?"

"I'm tellin' ya," Jerry said. "He's got men

152

who woulda been in and out with no problem, leavin' a dead broad behind." He shook his big head. "It ain't Mr. Giancana."

"How about somebody trying to get at him by killing the girl?"

Jerry sat back.

"She's here ta see Mr. S., right?"

"Right."

"And if they got it by Mr. Giancana, how could anybody else know?"

It seemed to me Jerry was saying that if MoMo didn't know, nobody did.

"Well, somebody sent those guys."

He shrugged.

"Maybe it ain't got nothin' ta do with Mr. Giancana at all. Maybe somebody else wants her dead."

"I wonder," I said, "if she's got another guy on a string, somebody who's not connected."

"If he ain't connected, how would he send those guys to kill 'er?"

"I'm just throwing stuff out here, Jerry," I said, "trying to see what fits."

He remained quiet for a moment, then said, "I don't like talkin' about Mr. Giancana. It ain't respectful."

"Okay, Jerry, then we won't do it anymore. I think you've already helped me, anyway. I mean, besides keeping me alive."

"I told ya I wouldn't let nothin' happen to ya."

"Yep," I said, "you told me that, and you're a man of your word."

We went out into the casino. I saw a guy at one of the roulette wheels who was a valet at the Riviera. He waved at me. At a black-jack table I spotted a girl who waited tables at the Palms. I got a smile. And at one point we passed a guy I knew who was a musician in one of the strip shows, who exchanged nods with me. I couldn't think which. I had a better memory for faces than I did for names, unless the person was somebody I thought would be useful to me.

"You know a lot of people in Vegas," Jerry said, "and not just celebrities, huh?"

"I like to know what's going on in town."

"You shoulda never left New York, Mr. G.," he said. "You'd have that town wired, too."

"Vegas is my town, Jerry," I said. "I was born in New York, but I'm glad to be out of there."

"Why'd ya leave —"

I cut him off. "You mind talking about those two dead hitters?"

"Naw," he said, "them I'll talk about, but I don't know nothin'."

"Just tell me why this guy would be sitting at one of my tables?" I asked, showing him the photo again.

"You still can't remember what he said to you?"

"No."

The time and date on the photo told me he'd been there the day before I talked to Frank. I mentioned that to Jerry. He took the photo and studied it.

"Maybe he was casin' you."

"Me?" I asked. "Why me? I wasn't even involved yet."

Jerry said, "Hey, Mr. G., I'm just throwin' stuff out there. . . ."

TWENTY-EIGHT

I decided Jerry was doing more than cracking wise. Why else would Joey Favazza have been in the Sands if he wasn't watching me? Coincidence? Then I did think of another possibility. Maybe he was tailing Frank, hoping he'd lead him to the girl.

"Jerry," I asked, "can you get me in to see Frank?"

"When?"

"Today."

"He likes me to check in," Jerry said. "I'll ask him."

"That's what I'd like you to do."

"Now?"

"There's a house phone right over there," I said. "Just pick it up and ask for his suite."

"Okay, Mr. G."

I watched as the big guy went to the phone, picked it up and spoke into it. It took a few minutes for the call to connect and then I assumed he was talking to Frank.

This way I didn't have to go and find Joey Bishop, or call Jack Entratter.

While Jerry was on the phone I walked over to the blackjack tables and watched some of the action. It wasn't my pit but I did recognize some of the players. The pit boss on duty was a guy named Barney Crane. He was an arrogant sonofabitch who nobody liked except, for some reason, Jack Entratter. I watched some of the hands being dealt, and I watched Barney, who didn't see me standing there.

When Jerry came back to join me I asked, "What's the word?"

"He said he has to go to the Fremont Theatre to rehearse with Mr. Martin and the others," Jerry said. "We can meet him there."

"When?"

"Now. He's takin' a limo over."

"Let's give him some time to get there," I suggested.

"What do we do until then?"

"We're gonna stand here and watch," I said.

"Watch what?"

"See that guy over there . . ."

We parked the Caddy behind the theater and walked around to the front. There was security on the door to keep the public out but I knew one of the guys — he had a marker at the Sands — and they let us in. We walked through the lobby to the theater and stood in the back for a while to watch.

Up on stage were Frank, Dino, Sammy Davis Jr., Joey Bishop and Peter Lawford. There were musicians in the pit, and some other people — men and women — standing around watching. Presumably, they all had reasons to be there, even if they were just Rat Pack hangers on.

Actually, the guys never did call themselves the Rat Pack. Frank hated the name. He called what they did The Summit, and was also known to refer to them as the Clan. The others didn't much care what they were called, they just wanted to have a good time and hang out with Frank.

They did a few numbers, checked the microphones to see if they were working; Joey did some jokes, the guys laughed, joked back. There actually wasn't much rehearsal to be done. While Joey Bishop did write a lot of the jokes, much of the shtick they pulled on stage was spontaneous. All of these guys were smart, funny, and had been on stage many times. Even Peter Lawford. Since the last time I met him I'd learned that before getting on stage with the Clan he had performed with Jimmy Durante. I'd always assumed he was just a pretty boy actor who wanted to hang around with Frank and Dean. Maybe I'd been wrong about him. He seemed to be able to carry his weight on stage.

Didn't mean I liked him any better, though.

We moved down one of the aisles so that Frank and the others could see us. That was when Frank told everyone to take five which, to Frank, meant about fifteen or twenty.

Dean waved at me from the stage and said, "Hey, pally." I felt a kind of ridiculous pride and sent a friendly wave back.

"What's up, Eddie?" Frank asked. "Jerry said you wanted to see me."

A look passed between him and Jerry and the big guy faded away. He didn't join the others by the stage, but moved several aisles away and sat down — uncomfortably, because the theater seats could not fully accommodate his bulk.

"We had some excitement last night," I said, and told him what happened.

"Jesus," Frank said, "every time I ask you to help somebody tries to kill you."

"Tell me about it."

"You want to pull out? No hard feelin's?"

159

"You know I don't, Frank," I said.

"Yeah, I do know, Eddie. You're a stand-up guy."

"And I'd like to stay that way."

"Whataya want me to do?"

"You ever hear of Joey Favazza or Frank Capistrello?" I asked.

"No," he said. "Those the two guys?"

"That's them."

He gave it another moment's thought, then said, "Sorry, neither of those names ring a bell."

"Do you think Giancana knows about you and Mary?"

"No," Frank said.

"You're that sure?"

"I told you, we've been discreet," he said. "MoMo doesn't know, Juliet doesn't know. . . ."

"And the rest of the guys?"

He shook his head.

"Nobody."

"Dean?"

He smiled. "Dino wouldn't approve."

"Frank," I said, "somebody sent two hit men to kill Mary."

"That doesn't make sense, pal," he said. "She's a sweet kid, never hurt anybody."

"Well, it's pretty damn sure she's on the

run now, or hidin' out. Has she tried to call you?"

"I told her not to call me at the Sands."

"If she was in trouble she wouldn't do it anyway?" I asked.

"You don't know 'er," he said. "She'd cut off her right arm first."

"She's that loyal?"

"I told you, she's special."

"But loyal to you? Not MoMo?"

"She wants to get away from him."

"And you're gonna help her? Go against Giancana?"

He pursed his lips, stroked them with a thumb and forefinger.

"I'm not gonna discuss that with you, Eddie. That okay?"

"For now, Frank," I said.

I thought he looked at me with new respect and felt another surge of silly pride.

"What else can I do?" he asked.

"I don't know, Frank," I said. "I really don't."

"What can you do?"

"I'm doing all I can. Look, one of these guys was in the casino the day before you and I talked."

"That's strange."

"He must have known you were gonna ask me for help," I said. "Who'd you tell?"

"Nobody," he said, an edge to his voice. "I told you, I didn't tell anybody about this."

We both knew he told Dino, who called Jerry. It was odd, though, how we both trusted the big lug.

"Well, somebody told somebody," I said.

He stared at me for a few moments, then said, "Mary? You think she told somebody?"

"Maybe she hasn't been as discreet as you," I told him.

"Nah —"

"A sister? A best friend?"

He pursed his lips, did the thing with his fingers again, thinking.

"What?"

"She's got a sister."

"Where?"

"In Chicago."

"Younger or older?"

"Older."

"They talk?"

"Well, yeah, they're sisters."

"What's her name?" I asked.

"Now wait a minute," he said. "I don't wanna bring her sister into this."

"If she's on the run, Frank, and she won't call you, who do you think she'll call for help?"

He hesitated, then said, "Lily."

"The sister?"

"Yeah."

"Give me her phone number, her address, any place that I can reach her."

He was wearing a sports jacket, no tie, like the rest of the guys on the stage. He took a pen from his inside pocket, but we had nothing to write on. Before either of us could move Jerry's big paw appeared with a small pad of paper.

"Thanks, Jerry," I said.

Frank wrote down what he knew and handed the pad back to me. I tore the sheet loose and handed the rest back to Jerry.

"I — I've got to get back to rehearsal," Frank said. It was the most upset I'd ever seen him. His Sinatra cool had been shaken.

"One more thing, Frank. Where does Giancana live?"

"MoMo has lots of places, but he's usually in Chicago."

"That's where he met Mary?"

"Yeah."

"And you, too."

"Yeah, at the Ambassador East. She was the hat check girl."

MoMo Giancana and Frank Sinatra sharing a hat check girl. Party girls like Judith Campbell and stars like Phyllis McGuire weren't enough.

"Do what you can for her, Eddie," Frank

said. "Find her. Keep her alive."

"That's what I intend to do, Frank."

Frank went back to the stage. I started up the aisle and Jerry caught up.

"Everything okay?"

"Like what?"

"I mean, between you and Mr. S.?"

I stopped and looked at Jerry, who went ahead a few steps before also stopping.

"What?" he asked.

I wondered what would happen if I told Jerry that everything wasn't all right between me and Frank? What would he do?

I didn't want to find out.

"Yeah, Jerry," I said, "everything is fine with me and Frank, just fine."

TWENTY-NINE

I needed access to a phone I could use to make a long-distance call. The nearest place to the Fremont Theatre was Danny Bardini's office. I figured he wouldn't be in — and he wasn't — but I knew where he kept a spare key.

"He won't be mad?" Jerry asked as I let us in.

"No, he won't be mad," I said. I was suddenly leery of Jerry, uncomfortable, even. "Jerry, why don't you go across the street and get us some coffee."

"And donuts?"

"Sure," I said, "get us some donuts, too."

"Okay, Mr. G."

I went to the window and watched the big guy cross Fremont Street. I was probably being silly. What could ever happen between me and Frank that would cause Jerry to have to take sides?

I went to the phone, fished out Lily

165

Clarke's phone number and dialed it. It was picked up on the second ring.

"Mary?" I could hear in that one word how frantic she was.

"Lily?"

Silence from the other end, and then, "Who is this?"

"My name is Eddie Gianelli, Lily," I said. "I'm calling from Las Vegas."

"Are . . . are you with the police?"

"No," I said. "I'm not with anyone. I'm just trying to find your sister and help her."

"I — I —"

"Have you heard from her?"

"I — I don't know you," she said. "I should hang up."

"Yes, you could," I said, "but you might be lousing up the only chance your sister has."

More silence, then she whispered, "I don't know what to do."

"Lily . . . is it Lily Clarke?"

"No," she said, "Lily D'Angeli. I was — I'm divorced."

"Can I call you Lily?"

"Mister — if you can help my sister you can call me anything you want."

"I'm trying to help her, but to do that I've got to find her."

166

"Do you know — have you been involved —"

"Are you asking me if I know what's going on out here?"

"Yes."

"To tell you the truth, I don't," I said. "I was asked to find her, and I walked straight into a mess. Two men are dead."

"Two?"

"Did she tell you about one?"

"She said — she said he tried to kill her."

"And she killed him?"

She didn't answer.

"Lily?"

"I think — I'm supposed to send some — I think I've said too much."

"Lily, remember my name," I said, speaking quickly so I could say what I wanted to say before she hung up. "I work at the Sands here in Vegas, tell her she can contact me there —"

There was a click and the line went dead. I thought about calling back but decided she probably wouldn't answer.

What had she said, "I think — I'm supposed to send some —" Send some what? Money? How? Western Union, maybe?

Jerry came in at that moment carrying two containers of coffee and a box of donuts. From the amount of powdered sugar on his face and chest he'd eaten one already.

"What's goin' on?" he asked, putting everything on Danny's desk.

I grabbed the coffee, opened the box and fished out a jelly donut. I decided to go ahead and tell him about the phone call.

"So you figure the sister is sending money?"

"That's about all she can do, except for flying out here."

"How would she send money?"

"Western Union."

"That a hunch?"

"It's about all I've got."

He picked out a long cruller and bit off about half of it.

"So how many Western Union offices you got in this town?" he asked with his mouth full.

"I'm not sure."

"We'd have to cover them all," he said. "You, me, the P.I. — what if there's more than three?"

"I guess we'll just have to find out," I said, but then I wondered how smart it would be for all of us to sit in a Western Union office. That would mean none of us was actually out looking for her.

Jerry and I both jumped when we heard a key in the lock and Danny came walking into the outer office.

"Don't scare him," I said to Jerry.

"Hey, Dick," he shouted, "we're in here!"

Danny came in carrying a container of coffee.

"Better be some donuts left," he said as he entered the office. "I stopped across the street and they told me some guy as big as King Kong bought the last cruller." He looked at Jerry. "I figured that had to be you, Gunsel."

"I ate it," he said, "but there's plenty of other stuff in there."

Danny walked to the desk and snatched a donut with sprinkles. From the look on Jerry's face that was going to be his next pick. If these two weren't careful they were going to end up friends.

"You wanna let me have my desk?" Danny asked me.

"Be my guest."

"What're you guys doin' here, anyway?" he asked, lowering himself into his chair.

"I had a call to make."

"Knowin' you it was long distance."

I told him about Mary Clarke's sister in Chicago, and the short, aborted conversation we had.

"Western Union, huh? Gotta be more

than one in this burg. We can't cover them all."

"How about the one closest to here?" I asked.

"That's gonna depend on whether she's alone or not. If somebody's helping her they'll know their way around."

"What'd you find out about that?"

"Three guys didn't show up for work," he said. "One was a kid valet who called in sick. I went to his house. He really is sick. His mother even let me look in on him sleeping in his room. Nice lady. She works at the Flamingo."

"And?"

"Second guy was a bellman. He'd be a good bet because he could've met up with her in the lobby, or just the hallway."

"Did you check him out?"

"That's next," he said.

"And the third guy?"

Danny scratched his nose, left a small glob of jelly there. He was a big boy, I thought, let him find out for himself.

"I thought maybe you and the palooka would want to check that one out."

"Why?" I asked.

"Who's a palooka?" Jerry demanded.

"Because," Danny said, "the third guy who didn't show up for work was our ol' buddy Dave Lewis, the house dick."

It was silent for a moment and then Jerry said, "Never did trust that prick."

THIRTY

As Danny had assumed, Jerry and I took the Caddy and drove to Dave Lewis' apartment on Decatur Street.

"He didn't fit my profile," Danny admitted, "but Dave's a letch. When he's not at work he spends all his time in strip clubs. He wouldn't be able to resist a babe like this."

"I didn't like that guy from the start," Jerry said again as we pulled up in front of the place.

Foot traffic was not heavy and we mounted the steps without running into anybody. There were six doorbells and Dave's name was next to one.

"If we ring it we'll warn him," Jerry said.

"Or if the girl is there we'll scare her," I said. "Can you open this door?"

He gave me a look and said, "Mr. G."

He leaned against the frame, did something I couldn't see and the door popped

172

open. I looked around, but there was no one. I stepped in behind him.

Dave Lewis had an apartment on the second of three floors. As we made our way up the creaking stairs I expected doors to open and tenants to peek out, but they never did. Apparently, Dave lived in a building where people had learned to mind their own business.

When we got to Dave's apartment I knocked and we waited. Jerry pressed his ear to the door.

"If the girl's in there she might be going out the fire escape," he said.

I pounded on the door.

"Mary," I shouted, "Mary, we're here to help you. Mary, my name is Ed—"

Jerry grabbed my arm. He looked at me and shook his head.

He did his magic with the door again, popped it open, and we went in. The first thing I saw was a woman's compact on the end table near the sofa. I pointed.

"Dave's not married," I said.

"Didn't look like the type to have a broad stayin' with him, either."

"Dave," I called out.

I was thinking — hoping — we'd find him in bed with the flu, or something. I never expected to find him on his bed, dead.

"Crap," I said.

Jerry went to the bed, leaned over and touched Dave, who was fully dressed. I couldn't see his head because it was hanging off the other side of the bed.

"Somebody clobbered him," he said. "Lots of blood on the floor here."

That was when the metallic smell hit me. My stomach got queasy.

"What the hell is goin' on?" I demanded, angrily. "Is it us?"

"Us?" Jerry frowned.

"Something about our chemistry. We start working together and people die?"

"Mr. G., people are gonna die no matter what you and me are doin'."

He was right, of course. I started to walk around the bed for a look but he stopped me with a firm hand against my chest.

"Ya don't hafta see that. Somebody pounded him real good."

"Let's look around," I said. "Maybe she's hiding."

"Like in a closet? Under the bed?"

We looked in both places, and the bathroom. We found women's toiletries there, and some items of clothing, but nothing else.

"She was here," Jerry said, "but she's gone."

"The question is," I added, "was she the one who killed him?"

"He was hit more than once," Jerry said. "Couldn't have been quiet. Wanna go door to door and see who heard somethin'?"

"Actually, I do," I said, "but . . . are we gonna call the cops first?"

"We'll get in lots of trouble, this time," he said. "Your buddy Hargrove will have a shit fit."

"Yeah, my buddy," I said. "You're the one he keeps haulin' away in cuffs."

"Right."

"Quick look around again."

"What are we looking for?"

"I don't know," I said. "Something helpful. A note? A phone number? Something."

"She ain't comin' back here, is she?" Jerry asked.

"Nope," I said, "I don't think she'll be coming back here."

THIRTY-ONE

We couldn't call the police. We'd both end up behind bars. That would be bad for Mary Clarke. She was still out there running for her life, and who was left to help her but us?

And, of course, it would be really bad for the two of us.

We were almost out the door when I noticed a Yellow Pages on the floor. It looked as if it had been knocked off the table, landing face down and spread open. When I picked it up I saw that it was open to the page for Financial Services. Someone had circled a Western Union location. I tore the page out and told Jerry, "Let's get out of here."

The hall was empty, and we didn't encounter anyone on the stairs or out front. Once we were in the Caddy with Jerry driving I asked, "How long do you think he was dead?"

"I ain't no detective, but there was still blood dripping from his head."

"You notice how quiet it was? Nobody in the halls, or even poking their heads out?"

"They musta heard the commotion and decided to stay inside."

"Good for us," I said. "We managed to get out of there without being seen."

"We hope."

I took the phone book page from my pocket.

"What's that?" he asked.

"Someone circled a Western Union office."

"Think that's where her sister's sending money?"

"It's the only lead we have." I gave him directions. "Let's check it out."

What happened seemed clear — as mud. Somehow Dave Lewis got Mary Clarke out of the hotel and into his apartment. What happened after that was anybody's guess, but it looked as if he'd tried to make her comfortable. Obviously, whoever was after her had somehow tracked her there. But as far as I could see there would have been no point in taking her. Why not just kill her along with Dave? So the fact that she was on the run again made her very resourceful

— or lucky.

We pulled up across from the Western Union office and turned off the Caddy.

"Now what?" Jerry asked. "Should we go in and ask if she's been there?"

I thought that over and said, "Why not?"

"You want me ta do it?"

"No," I said, opening the door, "you stay here. Remember what she looks like?"

"I remember," Jerry said. "You described her to me six times."

I crossed the street and entered the Western Union office.

"I'm here to pick up a check for my girlfriend," I told the clerk. "Mary Clarke?"

The clerk didn't move.

"I can't give that to anyone but her," he said, with a bored expression.

"Shit," I said, "I was trying to do her a favor."

"Yeah," the guy said. I wondered how many boyfriends he'd had trying to pick up a girl's check — to keep it, cash it and take it to a casino.

"Well," I said, "can you tell me if she picked it up yet?"

The guy acted put out, but he looked it up.

"No, it's still here."

178

"Came in from Chicago, right?"

"Yeah."

"Okay," I said, "thanks."

I left, trotted across the street and got back in the car.

"The money is still there."

"So we wait?" he asked.

"Yeah," I said, "we wait."

By the time they closed she still hadn't shown up. We went back to Fremont Street to eat at Binion's Horseshoe. From there I called Danny Bardini to come and join us.

Over hot roast beef sandwiches and fries we told Danny about Dave Lewis.

"Jesus," he said, "what the hell is goin' on?"

"Exactly," I said.

"You guys did the right thing gettin' out of there. Hargrove would have your asses."

"That's what we thought," I said. "Thanks for backing us up."

"There's no tellin' when his body'll turn up," Danny said. "Maybe an anonymous call to the cops is in order."

"They'll have to connect it to the missing girl," I said. "It's too much of a coincidence. Won't they haul us in, anyway?"

"Maybe," Danny said, "but you have alibis."

"Each other?" I asked. "You think Hargrove will see it that way?"

"Weren't you at the theater this morning talkin' with Frank?"

"Yeah, but —"

"From what the gunsel here said, Dave's body was pretty fresh. He was probably killed while you were with Frank."

"I think the dick has a point," Jerry said.

"Well," I said, "there were a lot of other people in the theater."

"So who makes the call?" Danny asked.

We all looked at each other.

"None of us," I said, then. "Somebody in that building will call."

"What makes you say that?" Danny asked.

"It was too quiet," I said. "Somebody must've heard us knocking but nobody opened their door to look. I'll bet after we left somebody got brave and called the cops."

"Well," Danny said, "I can find out if that happened. I'll be right back."

He got up, then looked at Jerry.

"I know how many fries I have left."

Jerry gave him the finger.

"You and him are getting along," I said.

"Don't tell the dick I said this, but he's okay."

"Yeah, I think so, too."

I didn't have many friends outside of my job. In fact, I didn't have much of a social life. That's not a complaint. There are few things I enjoy as much as my job. But when I did get away from the Sands, it was usually in Danny's company, which I enjoyed.

After a moment, Jerry eyed Danny's plate and asked, "Do you really think he counted his fries?"

"Oh, yeah," I said. "He'd do that. He hates sharing his food."

Jerry thought about that for a while, then reached over and took two fries from Danny's plate, despite the fact that he still had plenty of his own.

When Danny came back he said, "I got a contact at the paper. He says they sent a guy out on a story of a dead man found in his apartment on Decatur." He sat down and looked at me. "So you were right. It's been called in. Hargrove should be comin' for you guys soon."

"Let him try and find us," I said. We had to go back to the Sands, though. He'd probably be waiting for us there.

Danny started to eat, then looked at Jerry, stuck his hand out and said, "You owe me two fries, Gunsel."

The big guy looked at me, but I just

181

THIRTY-TWO

Jerry made a suggestion on the way home and I entertained it.

"If the cops are gonna look for us at the Sands why don't we go to your place?"

"They'll look there, too, eventually," I said. "And what about another hit man or two coming after me?"

"I can protect you better at your house. The hotel's too big."

He had a point.

"Okay," I said. He still had a bag with his things in the backseat. "Let's go to my place."

"Can we get somethin' ta eat on the way?"

"You're still hungry?"

He gave me a look of disbelief and said, "I only had one sandwich."

"Fine," I said. "What do you want to pick up? We'll take it home."

"Chinks."

"As it happens," I said, "I do know a place

183

that has good Chinese."

We pulled up in my driveway with two greasy bags of take-out cartons and two six-packs of Piels. Waiting for our order at the restaurant had made me hungry, as well. Being around Jerry was a bad influence on me. I figured by the time this was over I'd probably gain twenty pounds — or be dead. Might as well go ahead and eat.

We sat at the kitchen table and opened all the cartons. Jerry knew where I kept the plates and grabbed a few. Finally he cracked open two beers and put the rest in the freezer to get colder faster.

I filled my plate with fried rice, beef with broccoli, and lo mein and said, "You know, I'm just a pit boss. I don't know how you get used to the death."

"You askin' me if I'm used to it?"

"I guess I just assumed you were."

He chewed some shrimp, crunching the crispy noodles he'd crushed over it, and seemed to think over the comment.

"You either got to get used to it," he said, "or get to the point where you don't mind it."

"Aren't those the same thing?"

"Naw," Jerry said, "there's a little difference. You can get used to anything, even if ya mind it."

"And which point are you at?"

He shrugged. "I guess I'm used to it. People got to die sooner or later."

"Dave Lewis didn't die of natural causes, though," I said. "And he didn't choose to die."

"Maybe he did," Jerry said. "Maybe by helpin' the girl he chose it."

"That's pretty deep, Jerry."

"I ain't deep, Mr. G.," Jerry said. "I just see things the way they are."

"Maybe that's what deep means," I offered.

He crushed more noodles onto his plate.

Three beers each later the doorbell rang. Jerry put his hand in his coat and came out with his .45.

"The cops," I said.

"Maybe."

We stood up.

"Just keep that thing out of sight."

We left the kitchen and went to the front door. I looked out my window. Two bulky forms stood on my porch. I turned on the light and saw two guys who didn't look anything like cops.

"You know them?" I asked him.

We switched places and he took a look.

"Never seen 'em before," he said, "but they ain't cops. Their coats cost too much."

"And why are they wearing coats in Vegas?" I asked. August in Vegas, I could only think of one thing overcoats could be used for.

"They're carryin'," he said. "We can go out the back."

"What if we just answer the door and find out who they are?" I asked. "You can get the drop on them, right?"

"If that's what you want, sure."

"Okay, then," I said. "I'll open the door and you . . . you do what you do."

"Okay."

"Just don't shoot them."

"Not if I don't have to."

The bell rang again as I was opening the door.

"Can I help you gents?"

"Your name Eddie Gianelli?" one of them asked. He was clean-shaven and I could smell his cologne. He had the kind of face that needed to be shaved a couple of times a day.

"That's me."

"Somebody wants to see you," the other one said. He was the same age as his buddy, mid-thirties, a little smaller but still six feet.

186

They stood with their hands in their pockets.

"Who?"

"You'll find out," the first one said.

"I'm gonna need you boys ta take your hands outta your pockets," Jerry said from behind me.

Cologne guy looked at me and asked, "He got a rod on us?"

"He does."

"That ain't nice."

"People have been trying to kill us lately."

"We ain't here to kill nobody," the smaller one said.

"Then take your hands out of your pockets," I said, "and we'll talk."

They did as they were told, brought their hands out empty except for pinky rings.

Jerry came up right behind me so they could see his .45.

"But you are carryin', right?" he asked.

"We're carryin'," the second guy said.

"Hey," the first one said, "ain't you the Jew?"

"That's me," Jerry said. "Who're you?"

"Teddy Bats," he said. "You and me we did a thing together once."

Jerry was quiet, then said, "Oh yeah, I remember. Teddy Battaglia, right?"

"That's right." He nudged his partner.

187

"This is Jerry the Jew I tol' you about."

"Why's he got a gun on us, then?" the other one asked. "We're on the same side."

"Are we all on the same side, Jerry?" I asked.

"Yeah, we are, Mr. G."

"So the man who wants to see me would be . . ."

"That'd be my guess," Jerry said, lowering his .45.

"You wanna come with us?" Bats asked. "Or follow in your own car?"

I found the question encouraging.

"Why don't we follow so you won't have to bother bringing us back," I suggested.

"You're supposed ta come," the second guy said. "He ain't." He jerked his head at Jerry.

"I go where he goes," Jerry said, "or he don't go."

"Listen you Jew bast—"

"It's okay, Mikey," Bats said.

"I don't like —"

"I said it's okay."

Mikey fell silent.

Bats said, "We'll wait in our car for you to pull outta the driveway."

"Okay," I said. "I've got to get my keys."

"No problem."

The two of them turned and left. I

188

switched off the light and closed the door.

"Jerry," I asked, "am I right in assuming that we're going to see —"

"— Mr. Giancana," he finished. "Yeah, I think so."

"Is this safe?"

"Well," he said, "if they was gonna whack us they coulda done it now — or tried. And I don't think they'd be lettin' us take your car."

"Is there anything I have to do when we get there?" I asked.

"Like what?"

"I don't know, genuflect, kiss his ring?"

"Mr. G.," he said, "just be respectful. That's all he wants."

THIRTY-THREE

The house we followed Bats and Mikey to was a few blocks off the strip, a million-dollar place across the street from a popular golf course. That's all I'll say about where MoMo Giancana lived when he was in Las Vegas.

Giancana's nickname for many years was "Mooney," and that was what everybody called him from his years growing up in Chicago to his early years as a mob enforcer. However, when he became powerful enough he changed his own nickname to "MoMo," which some said stood for "Mo Money."

Jerry explained this to me in the car, as he gave me a crash course in how to speak to Sam Giancana.

"Don't ever call him Mooney," he warned. "He's killed men for that. In fact, don't even call him MoMo. You don't know him well enough."

"I've heard Frank refer to him as MoMo."

"He likes Mr. S."

"What do you call him, Jerry?"

"Me? I call him Mr. Giancana."

"Not Mr. G.?"

Jerry frowned at me and said, "You're Mr. G. Why would I call Mr. Giancana that?"

"Gotcha."

The house was in a gated community, so one of Giancana's boys had to get out of the car and arrange for the gate to be opened. He got back in and we followed him up a long driveway.

We all got out of the car and congregated in front of the house.

"I gotta frisk you," Bats told me.

"Go ahead," I said lifting my arms.

He patted me down, satisfying himself that I wasn't carrying a gun.

"Jerry," Bats said, turning to face the big guy.

"I'm carryin'," Jerry said. "You already know that."

"Yeah, I do," Bats said, "but I gotta take it from you. Nobody gets in to see Mr. Giancana carryin' a piece."

Jerry balked.

"Come on, Jew," Mikey said. "Give."

Jerry pointed a finger at Mikey and said, "You I don't like."

"I'm cryin'," Mikey said.

191

"Jerry . . ." Bats said, warningly.

Jerry looked at me so I nodded my head and he gave up his gun. Some power, I had.

Bats separated the gun and clip, put them in separate pockets of his coat.

"You'll get it back when you leave."

I hoped he meant *handed* back.

We all went into the house, where Bats and Mikey removed their coats and hung them on hooks. I'm no expert but even I could see the bulges their guns made under their suits. I was wearing a windbreaker, Jerry one of his own ill-fitting suits.

"That a Brooks Brothers?" Bats asked him.

"Yeah," Jerry said, sourly, "it just don't look like it when it's on me."

"Gorillas shouldn't wear suits," Mikey said.

Although he was more then six feet, and Bats was even taller, Jerry towered over both of them. I thought Mikey was playing with fire mouthing off to Jerry, but I didn't like him, so I didn't warn him.

"This way," Bats said. "Mr. Giancana is waitin'."

Jerry and I followed them down a long dark hallway, past a bunch of rooms that were all dark. It reminded me of a house that gets closed for certain seasons, when the occupants are away on vacation. I had no idea if Giancana was just using it, or if he actually lived there.

At the end of the hall we came to a pair of double doors. Bats knocked and opened one door. This room was well lit, and standing in the center of it was short, dumpy, homely Sam Giancana, the most powerful gangster in Chicago — and, some said, in America.

"Here's the pit boss, Mr. Giancana," Bats said. "And the Jew."

"Jerry," Giancana said, "nice to see you."

"Thanks, Mr. Giancana."

"This is Mr. Gianelli?"

"Yes, sir."

Giancana's suit was more expensive than anyone else's, and it fit him perfectly. Unfortunately for him, it didn't make him any taller — and yet, in many ways, he was the biggest man in the room.

"Mr. Giancana," I said. "Can I ask what I'm doin' here?"

"You're here so we can have a talk, Mr. — can I call you Eddie? That's your name, right? Eddie? Or Ed?"

"Eddie's fine."

"Bats, you and Mikey take Jerry to the kitchen. He can always eat."

I couldn't take my eyes off Giancana. By

the time I looked behind me they were gone and we were alone.

"Nervous, Eddie?"

"Yes, sir."

"Don't be," he said. "Care for a drink? I'm gonna have one."

"Bourbon."

"Good man."

He went to a side bar, built two bourbons and then walked across the floor to hand me one. He was half a foot shorter than me, yet my heart was racing. But then, it had been doing that a lot, lately. I hadn't yet stopped shaking from finding Dave Lewis' body.

"Have a seat, Eddie."

I was grateful for the invitation. My legs were kind of weak. I picked a plush chair and lowered myself into it. He chose another that was a little higher than mine. Subtle.

"We have mutual interests, Eddie, you and me."

"We do?"

"You know we do."

I sipped my drink.

"I'm talkin' about Mary Clarke."

"Mary . . ."

"Listen," he said, leaning forward, "I'm gonna make this easy for you. I know about Frank and Mary. I don't care. I like them both. Frank's a stand-up guy; Mary's a cute kid."

I wondered if I was hearing right. Frank was sleeping with MoMo's girl and he didn't care? For a panicky minute I wondered if Giancana knew I slept with Judy Campbell six months ago?

"Look at me, Eddie," Giancana said, sitting back. "I ain't no matinee idol. I'm not Dean Martin, right? But I got broads crawling all over me. What's one more? Mary worked for me and I liked her. Still do. I don't want anything to happen to her."

"Neither do I."

"See? Like I said, interests in common."

"I see." I didn't want to see. I didn't want to have interests in common with one of the most dangerous mob bosses in the country. I just wanted to find the girl and go back to my pit.

"Good," he said. "Then you won't mind filling me in on what's been happening?"

Filling him in? I gave it about a second of thought and then figured, where's the harm? He might even have something to suggest.

So I told him, adding in all the bodies that were involved.

"That's a lot of dead men," he said. "And no sign of the girl?"

"Nope."

He swirled the ice cubes left in his empty glass. Was he signaling that I should get him a refill? Wasn't I the guest?

"This don't sound good," he said, finally.

"I know it."

He wasn't looking at me. More like through me, but then he focused.

"She's on the run, and you gotta find her."

"Maybe you have some men you'd rather put on this —"

"No," he said. "All I have with me are those meatballs. I'd have to fly somebody in, and somebody would notice. I don't want anything to happen to Mary, Eddie, but I can't be involved. Frank is layin' low on this, right?"

"Right."

"Then it's all up to you," he said. "But you got Jerry to help out. He's a good kid."

"He's already saved my life more than once."

"See? He's valuable to have around, not those two *idioti*."

That was not a hard Italian word to translate.

"Finish your drink," he said. "You have work to do."

I finished, but I wasn't ready to leave. This was an opportunity too good to pass up.

"Mr. Giancana, do you know two men

196

named Capistrello and Favazza?"

"*Arrampicatori!*" he said, with distaste.

"I'm sorry."

He groped for the English translation.

"Upstarts! Wanna-be's, you know?"

"Yes, I know."

"Whoever sent them is not in my Family, Eddie," he said. "In fact, I don't know any of the *Famiglie* who would employ them."

"Then who's tryin' to kill her?" I asked. "And why?"

He walked over to my chair, patted me on the cheek and said, "That's what you're gonna find out. *Capice?*"

He took my right hand in a handshake, pulled me from my seat and walked to the door with me.

"Where are your parents from, Eddie?"

"Sicily," I said. "At least, my father was."

"And you grew up in Brooklyn?"

"That's right."

"Your father ever beat you?"

"He, uh, let me have it once or twice, to straighten me out."

"My father beat me every day," he said, with his hand on my shoulder. "Every day, rain or shine. You know what he said?"

"What?"

"It was for whatever I did that day that he didn't know about."

"Must've been tough." I meant the situation, but he misunderstood.

"He was," he said, "and he made me tough."

He opened the door for me.

"Good luck, Eddie. Find that girl and keep her safe, eh?"

"How do I — I mean, do you want to know when I do? Can I call —"

"You leave it to Jerry," he said. "He'll get word to me."

"Okay," I said. "Uh, thanks, Mr. Giancana."

"Eddie," he said, slapping me on the back. "Call me MoMo."

THIRTY-FOUR

When I came out of the room — study, library, sitting room, whatever it was — I found my way back to the front door. As I reached it Jerry came from another direction, followed by Bats and Mikey, who was cradling his hand, his face white with shock.

"What happened?" I asked.

"It was amazin'," Bats said. "Mikey wouldn't shut up, you know? Like before? The Jew reaches out real quick. I didn't see nothin', but I heard it! He just snapped Mikey's middle finger."

I looked at Jerry, who shrugged, looking bored.

"We have to get back," I said.

"Lucky you drove your own car," Bats said. "I gotta take Mikey to the hospital."

"Can we go now?" Mikey whined. "It hurts!"

"Snap!" Bats said, shaking his head. "Just like that."

"I need my gun," Jerry said.

"Oh, sure." Bats went to his coat, retrieved the gun from one pocket and the clip from the other. He handed both to Jerry, who joined them once again, then slid the gun into his holster.

"You know where's the nearest hospital?" Bats asked.

I gave him directions.

"Thanks."

Jerry and I left first, while Bats was helping Mikey with his coat.

"Snap, huh?" I said.

"He wouldn't shut up."

"What about the other guy?" I asked. "He keeps callin' you the Jew."

Jerry looked at me and said, "I am a Jew. I should snap his finger for that?"

When we got back to the house, it was dark. We hadn't left any lights on. As we got out of the car, Jerry eased his .45 from his holster.

"You think we need that?"

"I just wanna be careful."

We went to the front door, found it locked. I used my key to let us in and turned on a lamp near the door.

"Gimme a minute ta look around," Jerry said.

He took two and I stayed where I was until he got back. He'd already put his gun away.

"We're clear."

"I need some coffee."

"I'll make it."

We went into the kitchen.

"How'd it go with Mr. Giancana?" he asked, plugging in the percolator.

"Great," I said. "He told me I could call him MoMo."

"He musta liked ya."

"Oh yeah," I said, "we're crazy about each other."

He started the pot and then turned to look at me.

"Whataya so mad at?"

"People getting killed," I said, "a girl on the run. Frank hidin' from MoMo Giancana when he doesn't have to. I'm mad because I'm involved again, the cops are gonna want my ass and all I ever try to do is help."

"Mr. S. don't hafta hide from Mr. Giancana that he's sleepin' with his girl?"

"MoMo doesn't care," I said. "She's a sweet kid but to him she's just another skirt. He all but told me he didn't care if Frank was nailin' her."

"Then what's all the fuss?"

"Seems like everybody wants to help her," I said. "Even me, and I never met her."

"It don't figure." He shook his head. "Not if she's just another dame."

"Well, Frank seems to feel more strongly about her than that."

"Still don't figure to me," he said. "Mr. Giancana, Mr. S., they can get any broad they want. Marilyn Monroe too, I bet."

"Probably." I thought about Frank with Ava Gardner and Juliet Prowse. I thought about Angie Dickinson, wondered if she'd ever been with Frank. Then I wondered if she'd be at the premier.

"Maybe Frank likes this girl because she was just a hat check girl."

Jerry shook his massive head. The kitchen of my little house wasn't big at all, and he dwarfed it. When the coffee was ready he poured two mugs and sat across from me. It helped when he sat.

"You got her picture?" he asked.

I shook my head.

"Danny still has it. I've got to get it back. Why?"

"Just curious," he said. "I wanted to take a look."

"She's just a blonde, Jerry," I said. "That's all the picture shows."

"Then why are so many people gettin'

killed over her?"

"You know," I said, "that's what's keepin' me in this. Not so much wanting to find her alive but trying to figure out who wants her dead."

Jerry sat back in his chair and looked around the kitchen.

"We got any donuts or somethin'?"

THIRTY-FIVE

I woke the next morning wondering if I should tell Frank Sinatra that he wasn't doing anything behind Sam Giancana's back. But what would that accomplish? Would he feel foolish? Or lose interest? Maybe it was exciting because it was dangerous. Knowing that MoMo didn't care would take that away.

I showered, dressed casually — the one perk of being off the clock — and went downstairs.

"About time," Jerry said from the sofa. He slept there, but now he was sitting, fully dressed, just waiting. "I'm starvin'."

"Late night," I said.

"Sometimes I wonder about you, Mr. G.," he said. "Ain't no late nights in Vegas."

"Who told you that?"

"You did."

"Pancakes?"

"I thought you'd never ask," he said, coming up off the sofa eagerly.

I decided to take him to the Sands and feed him there. I just wanted some coffee.

"You probably get a lotta free meals at the casino." He sounded envious.

"Some."

He drove the route confidently, since he knew the way now.

"Jerry, you think Frank would want to know that MoMo's on to him?"

He thought a moment, then said, "I don't think Mr. S. would like feelin' stupid."

Frank had told me several times that he and Mary Clarke were being discreet. I wondered if he was doing that more for the public, Juliet Prowse, or MoMo Giancana?

"You're probably right," I said. "Let's keep it to ourselves."

"Gotcha."

I had Jerry take a detour by the Western Union office. According to the clerk my "girlfriend" had not picked up her money yet, and I still could not do it for her. I gave him my card, a ten-dollar bill and asked him to call me when she came in.

At the Sands I sat Jerry in front of the glass and brick partition that separated the diners from the cooks in the Garden Room

205

Restaurant, instructed the waitress not to charge him, and got a coffee to go for myself.

"You ain't gonna leave the building, are ya?" he asked me.

"Not without you, pal," I promised, slapping his big shoulder.

" 'Cause I know you ain't heeled," he said.

"I don't need to carry a gun when I've got you, Jerry."

"You got that right."

He was tucking a napkin in his collar when I left him.

Jack Entratter was in his office. His girl let me go right in. She didn't seem to approve of the fact that I had brought my own coffee. Or maybe it was that I hadn't brought some for anyone else.

"Jesus Christ, Eddie," he said, "tell me you had nothin' to do with Dave Lewis gettin' murdered."

"Dave's dead?"

"You'll need a better act than that for Detective Hargrove, my friend," he warned me.

"I'll work on it."

I sat across from him and reported what had happened.

"Sounds like you got a lead on your girl,"

he said. "What are you doin' here?"

"Jack, you got a man you can put on that Western Union office for me?"

"Why do you need a man?" he asked. "You got Jerry, don't ya? And yourself?"

"We're going to be busy with something else."

He frowned.

"What else is there for you to do?" he asked. "You've got to find that girl, Eddie."

"I know, I know . . . but I talked with MoMo last night."

He sat still in his chair, giving me the satisfaction of getting the very reaction I was after.

"You what?"

"Giancana sent for me last night."

"He's in town?"

"Yes."

His eyes flicked around his desk for a moment, as if he was searching for some elusive memo.

"What'd he want?"

"To tell me what a great job I was doing," I said. "Said he wants me to find the girl alive."

"Is he gonna give you some help?"

"No, he said what you said, I've got Jerry."

"Does Frank know he's here?"

"I doubt it."

"He's not comin' to the premier, is he?"

"He didn't confide in me, Jack," I said. "You know the kind of man MoMo is —"

"Why are you callin' him that?" he demanded.

I gave him an innocent look and said, "Well . . . he asked me to."

He went very still for a second time.

"He what?"

"He asked me to call him MoMo."

"Asked you," he said, "or told you?"

"Oh no," I said, "he definitely asked me to. Slapped me on the back, too. I think we're pals, now."

Jack Entratter thought this all over for a moment, then said, "Well, we gotta try to give Mr. Giancana what he wants, right?"

"That's right, Jack. Now, do you have a man you can put on that office?"

"I got somebody."

"And I want to be called as soon as she shows up. In fact, he can call here."

"That's fine."

"Good," I said, "because Jerry and I have some other leads to follow."

I started to get up.

"Hargrove wants to see you."

"When was he here?" I asked.

"He called," Jack said. "I arranged for you to go and see him. Better than him comin' here, tearin' the place up lookin' for you."

"I agree. Uh, did he mention Jerry?"

"He did. You better take him with you."

"Is he going to arrest us, do you think?"

"Not unless he's got a witness who saw you kill Dave Lewis." He leaned forward. "There's no such witness, is there, Eddie?"

"Nope," I said, "no witness."

"Good."

I turned to leave and he said, softly, "Eddie?"

"Yeah, Jack."

"Mr. Giancana . . . he didn't say what he was doin' in Vegas, exactly . . . did he?"

"No, Jack," I said, "he didn't tell me that."

"Okay . . . thanks."

I left him sitting behind his desk, looking more worried than I'd ever seen him.

THIRTY-SIX

I truly believed that the only person Jack Entratter was afraid of was Sam Giancana. On a strictly physical level, of course, Jack could crush MoMo, but there was something much more going on.

I was initially impressed with Frank and Dino because of their celebrity. Later, I became more impressed with them because of their loyalty to each other. I could've been afraid of Jerry simply because of his size, but he had proven to me more than once that he was about much more than size. I felt that we were friends.

Sam Giancana scared me. Why? Because on his word alone my friend Jerry would probably take me out. That made him — not Jerry — the frightening one. On his say-so Jerry would probably even take out Frank Sinatra. One man shouldn't have that much power. The power to frighten somebody like Jack Entratter, or to snuff out lives like Frank Sinatra, or just me.

On the other hand, what had MoMo shown me by saying he didn't care if Frank was sleeping with Mary? Was he a man void of petty jealousy, or were women just not that important to him? And if so, why did he care what was happening to her now?

To get to the casino I had to take the elevator down and pass the front desk. On my way I heard somebody call my name. I turned and saw Charlie Slater, one of the concierges, waving me over to his desk.

"Yeah, Charlie?"

"There was a girl here lookin' for you earlier, Eddie," he said.

"A girl?"

"Well, a woman," he said. "A looker, too."

"What did she want?"

"She didn't say."

"What *did* she say?"

"She asked if a man named Eddie Gianelli worked here. I said you worked in the casino."

"Did she check in?"

"Not that I know of."

"When was this?"

"About an hour ago."

"I'll be in the building for another hour or so," I said. "In the casino. If she comes back, page me."

211

"You got it."

"Thanks."

I went to find Jerry. He was just outside the Garden Room, watching the blackjack players. I hoped he wasn't going to get hooked. He was a very good handicapper of horses but I didn't know how he'd handle having his twenty beaten so many times by the dealer's twenty-one. That takes a special kind of temperament. From my pit I've seen gamblers who were very good at other games — craps, roulette — have meltdowns at the blackjack table.

I sidled up next to him and asked, "What do you think?"

"About what?"

"About blackjack?"

He seemed to give it some thought, then said, "I think I'll stick to horses."

"Probably a good idea."

He looked at me.

"You think I ain't smart enough?"

"Smart's got nothing to do with it," I said. "I'm one of your biggest fans, Jerry. No, I just think you're better suited for the horses. And you're good at it. If you try to learn blackjack and become good at that, it could mess you up for the horses."

"Cards ain't for me," Jerry said, "but it's interestin' to watch."

I didn't think much of blackjack as a spectator sport. Poker maybe, but not blackjack.

"So what's goin' on?" he asked.

I told him I'd gotten Jack Entratter to send someone to the Western Union office to watch for the girl.

"He won't know what to look for."

"A hot blonde," I said. "That's all he needs to know."

"And if she shows up? Will he grab her?"

"He'll call Jack."

"He should follow her."

I mentally kicked myself for not having suggested that.

"Wait here," I said.

I went to a house phone and called Jack.

"Some detective," he said, when I told him. "You should get lessons from your friend Bardini. I already sent Franco, told him to follow her if she shows up and then call in."

I hung up, feeling properly chastised, and went back to Jerry.

"Taken care of," I told him.

"So what are we gonna do?"

"We have to go talk to Detective Hargrove."

"Do I have to?"

"Yes," I said. "If you don't he'll put out a

213

dragnet for you."

"I don't like police stations." He made a face and actually shivered.

"It'll be okay," I said. "We'll look better going in willingly."

"Now?"

"No," I said, "not now. I heard there's a woman here looking for me."

"What for?"

"I don't know," I said, "but I'm wondering . . ."

"Wondering what? If she's involved?"

"Maybe it's her," I said. "The concierge said she was a looker."

"A blond looker?"

"He didn't say. I just want to stick around another hour or so, see if she finds me."

Jerry shrugged and said, "Okay."

"You want to play the horses while we're waiting?"

"Why not?"

He knew how to get to the race and sports book, so he went off alone.

THIRTY-SEVEN

I had second thoughts about the identity of the woman looking for me being Mary Clarke. Why would she come to the Sands asking for Eddie Gianelli? I just couldn't buy that this girl who was on the run, who had probably escaped death at least twice, would still strive for discretion and not try to get in touch with Frank.

Then I thought about Frank's man, George Jacobs. Could he have intercepted a message from the girl and kept it from Frank?

"Eddie?"

I turned at the sound of my name. I hadn't moved from the spot where I'd been standing with Jerry. A bellmen stood patiently by. I tried to bring his name to mind but couldn't so I just raised my eyebrows at him.

"Uh, Charlie said for me to tell you that woman is back?"

"The one looking for me?"

He shrugged. "That's the message he gave me."

"Okay, thanks."

He went off to deliver another message somewhere else and I headed for the lobby. As I arrived I saw Charlie lean over and speak to a woman who was standing by his desk. She turned her head to observe my progress across the floor to her.

I took the time to look her over and I liked what I saw. She could have gotten a job in any of the casino shows based on her looks alone.

When I reached her, her lips parted slightly. The bottom one trembled before she could catch it. She was wearing a purple suit that was wrinkled, as if she'd traveled a long way in it — which she probably had. If she'd had blond hair she would have been a double for her sister.

"Miss D'Angeli?"

She seemed taken aback.

"H-how did you know?"

"You resemble your sister."

"She's a year younger," she replied, "but yes, we look alike. Are you the Mr. Gianelli I spoke to on the phone?"

"Yes," I said. "You got here quickly."

"And expensively," she said. "Can we talk?"

"Of course," I said, "but first . . . where are you staying?"

"I — I don't know. I came straight here from the airport. I — I checked my bag, but —"

"Come with me," I said. "We'll get you a room."

"I can't afford to stay here —" she said, as I took her arm.

"Don't worry about that."

"Oh, I couldn't —"

"We don't have time to argue, Miss D'Angeli," I said. "We'll get you a room and then we'll talk. No arguments."

"I — well, all right."

I took her to the desk and had them put her in one of the rooms the Sands kept open for employees, like me. Not a suite, but a decent room. Then we retrieved her bag and I took her upstairs. I carried her bag into the room, leaving the door open.

"Would you like to freshen up?" I asked.

"Do I have time?"

"You can take a few minutes," I said. "I'll wait out in the hall. Are you hungry? We could talk in the coffee shop."

"Well — yes, I'm very hungry. You're very . . . kind."

"Not what you expected?"

"I — I didn't expect —"

"Never mind," I said. "I'll wait outside."

I backed out and closed the door softly.

"After I hung up on you," she said, later, "I realized I might have just hung up on the only person who could help me — help Mary. I — I'm sorry I did that."

"It's okay," I said. "You didn't know who I was."

I paused while the waitress placed a salad in front of Lily D'Angeli. Instead of taking her to the coffee shop I chose the Terrace Room, one of the better restaurants in the building. In addition to the classy ambience it had a view of the pool.

"You're not having anything?" she asked. She had a Chicago accent, though not a broad one.

"I'm not hungry," I said. "Go ahead, eat."

I had a cup of coffee in front of me and the waitress refilled it. I thanked her.

"Have you heard from my sister?" she asked.

"I was going to ask you the same thing."

"Not since she called and I sent her that money," she replied.

"She hasn't picked it up yet."

She stared at me, chewing slowly, a dab of

French dressing at the corner of her full lips.

"How could you know that?" she asked. "I mean, how could you know where I sent the money?"

"We found where your sister was hiding, at least for a while. There was a Yellow Pages there with the location circled."

I didn't bother telling her that there was a dead man there, as well.

"I've got someone watching the place, waiting for her."

"To do what?"

"To help her," I said. "To bring her in and put her somewhere safe. Someone's trying to kill her, Miss D'Angeli. I don't want to see that happen."

"Why not?" she asked. "Are you being paid? You're not a detective, are you?"

"No," I said, "as I told you on the phone I work here. I'm a pit boss."

"I'm sorry," she said, shaking her head. "I don't know what that is."

"Maybe I'll tell you later," I said. "Right now I need to know why you came out here, Miss —"

"Please," she said, "after all you've done, please call me Lily."

"Okay, Lily," I said. "I'm Eddie. What I

219

want to know is, what are you doing here in Vegas?"

"I came to help."

"How?"

She stared at me for a moment. The dressing was still there, but as if she'd caught me looking, her tongue flicked out and nabbed it.

"I don't really know," she said. "After I hung up on you . . . rudely . . . I just reacted. I went to the airport, bought a ticket on standby and here I am."

She had a beautiful, clear complexion that was drawn now, etched with fine lines and some darkness beneath her eyes. She'd obviously spent the night at the airport.

"I've only seen a photo of your sister," I said, "but if you bleached your hair —"

"I wouldn't," she said, touching her brown locks. "She asked me to go with her and get it done at the same time but I said no. That was right after she got the job at that . . . that place."

"The Ambassador East?"

She nodded.

"Where all the gangsters go."

"And movie stars."

"To her they were the same."

A lot of people felt that way.

"She took that job, said she was going to

meet a rich man."

"I'll bet she met plenty."

"Yes," she said, "and she . . . she took money from them."

Not just for checking their hats, she meant.

"And I told her not to come out here when that . . . that singer invited her."

That singer?

"You don't like him?"

"I don't like his type," she said. "I'm not a big fan of people who think they're powerful."

"Like show business people?"

She nodded. "And gangsters, politicians . . . they're all the same."

"Do you want something else?"

She looked down at her salad as if she was surprised she'd finished it.

"No, no," she said, "that was fine. Thank you. Can I pay —"

"No," I said, "all part of the service."

Thirty-Eight

An hour later we were still in the Terrace Room. Her plate had been cleared away and we'd gotten her a cup of tea. I was still getting refills on my java.

"Can I ask why you have different last names?"

"Mary said she wanted something less ethnic. I think she just didn't want the same last name as me."

"I don't know," Lily said. "I just don't know who'd want to hurt her."

"There must be something she said," I prodded, "some hint that she knew why someone wanted to kill her."

"My sister was very secretive," she said.

"But she told you about Frank Sinatra."

"She was bragging. She liked to brag."

"Why!?"

"Because she knew my life was boring."

"And she liked to rub it in?"

"What she didn't understand was that I

never craved excitement like she did," Lily explained. "I like my life the way it is."

"What do you do?"

"I'm a bookkeeper."

"I see." I knew firsthand that was not an exciting life.

"No," she said, "you don't. You live . . . here, with all the lights and the glamour. You're like her. You can't understand how I'd be happy with what I have."

"I think I can, Lily," I said, "but that's not important. What's important is that you think back over recent conversations with your sister. There's got to be something she said that would give us a clue about who's tryin' to kill her, and why?"

"You keep saying that, but —"

"There you are."

Danny Bardini stood looking down at us. He was speaking to me, but smiling at Lily. She glanced up at him and immediately touched her hair. That's how it was with Danny and women — especially good-looking ones.

"Hey, Danny," I said. "This is Lily D'Angeli; she's Mary Clarke's sister."

"Ah," he said, "nice to meet you, Miss D'Angeli.

"Lily, this is Danny Bardini," I said. "In addition to being a good friend of mine, he's a private detective who's helping me look for your sister."

"Oh, well, thank you, Mr. Bardini," she said. I was sure the lilt in her voice was uncontrollable. I'd seen him do that to women before. "Can you join us?"

"Of course," he said, pulling out a chair. "I was looking for my friend, here, but I didn't expect to find him in such lovely company."

She blushed.

"What's up, Danny?" I asked.

"Well, I wish I could tell you I had somethin' on the girl," he said, then quickly added, "Sorry, on your sister, Miss D'Angeli."

"Please, call me Lily."

"What do you have something on, then?" I asked.

"Dave Lewis," Danny said. "Looks like he got on the wrong side of some people."

"You're saying maybe his getting killed had nothing to do with Mary?"

"That's what I'm sayin'."

"Killed?" Lily asked.

Danny looked at me.

"When I told you we found where your sister was hiding I didn't tell you the whole story, Lily," I said. "The man who was hiding her got killed."

"Oh, God . . ." She picked up a napkin and began shredding it.

"Now it looks like it might not have had anything to do with your sister."

"You mean . . . it was just a coincidence?"

"Could be," Danny said.

I told Danny that we had a man watching the Western Union office where Lily had sent Mary money.

"She probably won't go near it," he said. "Too scared."

"How would she get money, then?"

Danny and I exchanged a glance. There were a lot of ways a blond babe could make money in Las Vegas.

"Maybe she'd panhandle," Danny said, picking the lesser evil. "You know, beg on the street?"

"Oh no," she said, "Mary would never do that."

I knew Danny and I were wondering the same thing — did Lily really know what her sister might do if she was desperate enough?

"Listen, I forgot to give this back," Danny said. He pulled the photo from his pocket and was about to hand it over when he looked at it. He froze, then looked at Lily.

"Yes, I know," she said.

"We already went through this," I told him, taking the photo.

"Eddie, you haven't told me why you're so interested in helping my sister?" Lily asked. "I mean, initially, how did you become involved?"

"I thought I might have told you that on the phone," I said. "I was, uh, asked to see if she was okay when she was, uh, unreachable."

" 'Unreachable?' Oh, you mean, when he couldn't get her on the phone?"

"Yes." I told her how I went to the hotel, got into her room and what I found there. Then we told her about Dave Lewis, and how we figured they must have hooked up.

"Poor Mary," she said, when I was done. "Not only is someone trying to kill her, but she ends up being helped by a man somebody wants to kill."

"Where's big Jerry?" Danny asked.

"Playing horses."

"Jerry?"

"Another friend of mine is helping out."

"My," she said. "Mary has all these men trying to find her and help her."

"And you," Danny said. "Don't forget she has you."

"I'm afraid I won't be very much help," she said. "I'll probably just be in the way, but I had to fly out here."

Danny put his hand on hers, stopping her

from further tearing an already destroyed napkin.

"I'm sure you'll be very helpful," he said.

"I can't see how."

"Well," he said, "if we get in touch with her maybe she'll come in because you're here."

"How will we get in touch with her?"

"There's only one person in town she'll call, if she gets desperate enough."

"That singer?" she asked, with distaste.

Danny looked at me. I knew what he was thinking. Maybe not liking Sinatra was the only flaw she had.

"I want to ask him about it," I said, looking at my watch, "but I'm due to go and talk to the police."

"The police?"

"About Dave Lewis," I said. "Jerry and I have to go and talk to Detective Hargrove. Danny, would you see Lily back to her room?" I looked at her. "Or would you like to gamble a bit? I can arrange —"

"Oh, no," she said, quickly, "I'm not a gambler."

"How about a show?" I asked before I could stop myself.

"No, thank you. I think I'd just like to go to my room and get some rest. I'd also like to be there in case something . . . happens?"

227

"We'll make sure you know everything that happens," Danny said. "Won't we, Eddie?"

"We sure will, partner."

I signed the check and we left together.

"I've got to go get Jerry," I said. "Lily, I'll call you as soon as I get back. Danny?"

"I'll keep Lily company."

Not in her room, I thought as they walked to the elevators. Unless I missed my guess, I thought Lily was just a little too prudish for Danny to be able to work all his magic on her.

Thirty-Nine

Detective Hargrove did not have an office of his own so he took us into an interview room. I could see Jerry was very uncomfortable.

Hargrove sat across from us while his partner, Gorman, stood leaning against a wall with his arms folded across his chest.

"Your buddy Dave Lewis is dead," Hargrove said.

"I'm sorry to hear it."

"But this isn't the first time you're hearing it, is it?"

"No," I admitted, "I knew it before we came in here."

"How?"

I shrugged. "Word gets around."

"No," Hargrove said, "I want to know exactly who told you."

"Jack Entratter," I said, without hesitation. No harm there. It was Jack who arranged for us to come to Hargrove instead of the other way around.

"And you didn't know before he told you?"

"No."

"What about you?"

Jerry inclined his head towards me and said, "He told me."

Hargrove stared at Jerry, who glared right back.

"You didn't walk in here with a gun, did you, big guy?" Hargrove asked.

"I got a permit."

"See if he's got his gun on him," Hargrove told his partner.

Gorman left his position against the wall and approached Jerry, who stood and raised his arms. Gorman patted him down.

"He's clean."

"Why didn't you just say so?" Hargrove asked.

"And ruin your fun?"

"Wise guy."

Jerry didn't respond. In fact, he might have taken the remark as a compliment.

Hargrove looked at me.

"Do you know if Dave Lewis had a woman living with him?"

"I didn't know him that well."

"You don't know if he liked women?"

"Oh, he liked women," I said. "I just don't

know if he lived with one."

"Well, we found some women's things in his apartment," Hargrove said.

"Clothes? Makeup? Those kinds of things?"

"Yeah, those kinds of things. We think maybe that's where the missing woman, Mary Clarke, was."

"So you don't think she's dead?"

"On the run maybe," he said. "Not dead, although she seems to be leaving dead men in her wake."

"In her wake?" I asked. "You should be a writer, not a cop."

He stared at me.

"Maybe she left a dead man behind in her hotel room," I said, "but you can't prove she was ever in Dave's place."

"That's true."

I was waiting for Hargrove to ask me the question he hadn't asked yet, the one where I'd either have to lie or give up Frank Sinatra's name. But he didn't ask, and I wondered if that was Jack Entratter's doing?

"Eddie, you got anything on this missing girl?" Hargrove asked.

"Like what?"

"Like I know you and your friend Bardini are looking for her," he said. "You got any leads?"

I thought about denying I was looking for her, but that would've been foolish.

"No, we've got nothing," I said. "If she was with Dave Lewis I wish I'd known about it."

"Your high roller hasn't heard from her?"

"Not a peep."

"Bet he's glad."

"Why?"

"All these bodies, that's a lot of scandal," Hargrove said. "He wouldn't want to have to deal with all that, would he?"

"I wouldn't know," I said. "I'm just supposed to see what I can do to help find the girl."

"Well, you keep doing that, Eddie," he said. "You and big Jerry, here. See, we're just a bunch of dumb cops and we need all the help we can get."

"Hey," I said, standing up, "that's why we came down here. To help."

Jerry stood up with me.

"If there's anything else we can do for you, let us know," I said. "Are we free to go?"

"Sure, why not?" Hargrove asked. "Get out of here."

We headed for the door.

"One more thing," Hargrove called out.

We stopped and turned.

"Where were you when Dave Lewis was

getting himself killed?"

"Am I supposed to know when that was without you telling me?" I asked.

Hargrove stared at me, then waved a hand dismissively and said, "Get the hell out of here."

Outside the building I asked Jerry, "Where the hell is your gun?"

"In your car."

"In my car?" I asked. "My car that's parked in front of a police station?"

"Relax," he said. "They ain't gonna search your car. They only frisked me to piss me off."

When we got to the car he sat behind the wheel and I got into the shotgun seat — no pun intended.

"Where is it?" I asked.

"Glove compartment."

He started to reach and I said, "Not here, for Chrissake."

He gave me a pitying look, as if he felt sorry for me because I was so nervous. I didn't tell him that he'd looked pretty uncomfortable in there, himself.

FORTY

George Jacobs and I had talked once or twice, but never about Mary Clarke. I asked Jerry how much of Frank's business he thought George knew.

"Most of it," he said, "maybe all. He's on the inside, so he hears everything. Why?"

"I think I want to talk to him about this whole missing girl thing."

"George ain't got nothin' ta do with it," Jerry said. "I can guarantee that."

"How?"

"He's loyal to Mr. S."

"That may be," I said, "but it also may be he's heard something he doesn't even know he heard."

Jerry shook his head and said, "I don't think you'll get nothin' outta him."

"Well, we've got a little over forty-eight hours before the premier," I said. "I think Frank wants this off his mind by then, and the only way that's going to happen is if we find the girl."

"I still don't think you're gonna get nothin' from him," Jerry said, "but I guess it don't hurt ta ask."

Jerry called Frank's suite from the lobby. Frank wasn't there, but George was. Jerry told him we were coming up.

George Jacobs was a handsome black man whose age was hard to gauge. There was some salt in his black hair, so my best guess would have put him about the same age as Frank.

"Mr. Sinatra won't be back for a while," he told us as we entered. "He's rehearsing."

"That's okay, George," I said. "I wanted to talk to you."

"To me, sir?"

"That's right. Why don't you sit down?"

"Sit down?" George asked, looking puzzled. I wondered when the last time was that someone invited him to sit down. "But . . . can I get you something, sir? A drink?"

"Jerry can get us all something," I said. "How about it, Jerry?"

"Sure," Jerry said, moving towards the bar. "Whataya have?"

"Oh . . . I couldn't do that, sir," George said, still standing.

"Come on, George," I said. "You mean to tell me you don't have a little sip when Frank's not around?"

"I don't drink Mr. S.'s stock, sir," George said, stiffly.

"Hey, George," I said, "come on, I was just kidding. Seriously, have a seat. I've got some questions I want to ask you, and I think you know that Frank — Mr. Sinatra — would want you to answer them."

"That would depend on what they are, sir," he said, but finally sat down on the edge of an armchair.

I heard Jerry open a beer and waved one off. He stood behind the bar and drank his.

"George, you're Frank's Man Friday, aren't you?" I asked.

"I prefer the term 'valet,' sir."

"As his valet then, how much do you know about what goes on in your boss's life?"

"I assume everything, sir."

"Does anybody really know everything?"

"I do, sir," he said, proudly.

"Good, then you know all about Mary Clarke?"

"It wouldn't be right for me to answer that, sir."

I knew this wouldn't go well if I couldn't loosen him up a bit.

"George," I said, "Frank has asked me for my help. You know that, right?"

"Yes, sir."

"Then that means he wants you to help me."

"That would depend, sir."

I looked over at Jerry.

"You want me to beat it outta him?" he asked.

George looked concerned — not scared, but definitely concerned.

"No, Jerry," I said. "Nobody's getting beat up."

Jerry shrugged, as if he could care less, and drank some more beer.

"George, I'm just gonna have to ask you straight out: do you know anything about the disappearance of Mary Clarke?"

"No, sir, I do not." I was pleasantly surprised by his answer. No more beating round the bush.

"Do you know if she's spoken to Frank since the night she disappeared?"

"Not to my knowledge, sir."

"But you said you knew everything."

"If she and Mr. S. have spoken since that night, I believe I would know it, sir."

"Even if Mr. Sinatra was being extra careful with this girl?" I asked.

237

George frowned. "And why would that be, sir?"

Did I want to say Giancana's name to George? Actually, I didn't want to say it to anyone.

"Juliet Prowse, for one."

He still hadn't admitted he knew anything about Frank and Mary Clarke.

"Miss Prowse will be coming to the premier, sir," he said, instead. "She will be on Mr. S.'s arm. That is all I know."

That was all he was saying.

"Okay, George," I said. "You're loyal to Mr. Sinatra. I understand that."

"Thank you, sir." He looked over at Jerry, as if he thought I might still unleash the big man on him.

"Jerry, let's go."

"He ain't admitted nothin'," Jerry said.

"That's okay," I said. "We're done here."

Jerry shrugged, left the remainder of his beer on the bar for George to clear away, and followed me out into the hallway.

"I told you he didn't know nothin'."

"He's just not saying, Jerry," I said. "It's not the same thing."

We walked to the elevator. Once inside and on the way down I asked, "Would you have beaten it out of him if I told you to?"

He shrugged and said, "That's my job."

FORTY-ONE

I took Jerry to the lounge and bought him a beer. While we drank I told him about Mary Clarke's sister.

"Good-lookin' as her?" he asked.

"Yeah, but without the blond hair."

"Bet your P.I. buddy's givin' it to her right now," Jerry said. Most guys would have leered while they said it, but he didn't. He was just making an observation.

"I don't think so."

"Why not?" he asked. "Seems to me he's the type."

"Oh, he's the type, all right," I said. "But she's not."

"Mr. G.," he said, "they're all the type."

"Not this one," I said. "Pure Midwest."

"I got a question for ya," Jerry said.

"Shoot."

"That cop," he said, "why ain't he askin' who you were workin' for when you went lookin' for the girl?"

239

"You know, I've asked myself that same question."

"Come up with any answers?"

"Two," I said. "One, he's too dumb, and I don't think he is, and two, he's been told not to."

"By who?"

"That's part of the same question."

"His boss?"

I shrugged. "Maybe your boss."

Jerry didn't comment. I still wasn't all that sure who his real boss was. Probably some New York counterpart of MoMo.

"Maybe mine," I said, thinking about Entratter. Did he have that kind of power?

"I can think of another reason," Jerry said.

"Let me have it, then."

"Maybe," he said, "he already knows."

We were about to leave the lounge when a bellman entered, spotted me and came over.

"Message for you, Mr. Gianelli."

"Thanks."

"What is it?" Jerry asked.

I unfolded it and read.

"Jack says the girl still hasn't picked up the money, and the office closed."

Jerry ran his finger around the rim of his empty beer glass.

"She must be dead, Mr. G.," he said.

240

"Why else would she not pick up the money? She needs it bad."

"Maybe she can't get to it."

" 'Cause she's dead."

"Or being held."

He shook his head. "She ain't bein' held by nobody."

"Why do you say that, Jerry?"

"Because she's marked," he said. "There's a hit out on her. There's guys out there with a reason to kill her, but ain't nobody got a reason to just take 'er and hold 'er. See what I mean?"

"I see, Jerry," I said. "I see."

"Where we sleepin' tonight, Mr. G.?" he asked.

"Where are we safe, Jerry?"

He shrugged and said, "You're pretty much safe where I am."

"What if there's a hit out on me?"

"There ain't."

"You know that for a fact?"

"That guy I shot in your room? He was here for the girl, not you. You was just a way for him to get to the girl. Nobody's tryin' ta hit you, Mr. G. At least, not for money."

I didn't find that comforting at all.

FORTY-TWO

When we left the lounge I took Jerry over to watch some blackjack. He watched the players, and I watched the dealers and Barney Crane. Crane was giving me one of his arrogant sonofabitch looks when somebody poked me in the back . . . hard.

I turned and saw Detective Hargrove standing there, his face a rosy glow that didn't come from the casino lighting.

"You and me have to talk," he said. "Alone."

Jerry turned and glared at the detective.

"Turn it off, torpedo," Hargrove said. "Your bad looks don't scare me."

"He doesn't like to be called that," I said.

"Too damn bad." He jerked his thumb at Jerry. "Get lost."

"I got a better idea, Detective," I said. "Let's you and me get lost."

"Someplace quiet," Hargrove said to me.

"Coffee shop's quiet," I said. "And I'll buy

242

you something to eat."

Hargrove glared at me, then said, "Normally I'd tell you to shove it, but I'm hungry."

Quickly I stepped over to Jerry and said, "I want you to do me a favor."

"What?"

"See that guy behind the tables? In the pit?"

"The guy you don't like."

"That's right," I said. "I want you to just stand here and stare at him."

"That's it?"

"That's it," I said. "Just fold your arms and stare at him until I come back."

"Okay, Mr. G." He was puzzled, but he agreed.

I turned to Hargrove and said, "Come this way."

We walked through the casino towards the coffee shop. To my complete shock I saw Angie Dickinson walking towards us. She was dressed for a night out, her off-the-shoulder gown showing just enough cleavage and leg to entice, but no more, because she was so sensual she didn't need to flaunt acres of skin.

As we passed she smiled at me and said, "Hello, Eddie."

My mouth was too dry to say anything, so I just nodded and continued to watch as she walked away from us. I noticed that Hargrove was watching, as well.

"T-that was Angie Dickinson," he said.

"She must be here for the premier," I said, as nonchalantly as I could.

"She knows you?"

"We've met," I said. "Come on, coffee is this way."

Having Angie Dickinson know me by name was just another reason for him to hate me.

He grabbed a menu and ordered an open-faced roast beef sandwich, mashed potatoes and a glass of water.

"Sure you don't want something stronger to drink?" I asked.

"Fuck you, Eddie," he said.

I looked up at the startled waitress and said, "Nothing stronger for the gentleman. I'll just have some coffee."

As she walked away, shaking her pretty head, I said, "You shocked the young thing."

"I'm sure she's heard worse working here."

"Tell me, Detective," I said, "did I do something to you last time to make you hate me, or do you hate everybody?"

"Not everybody," he said. "Just mugs like you and your pal Jerry."

"Me and Jerry," I said, "we're nothin' alike."

"You're more alike than you want to admit, Eddie," he said. "Maybe you fool yourself, but you don't fool me. You work for the mob, you're in with the mob."

"I'm a pit boss," I said. "I work in a casino."

"Yeah," he said, "that's why you're out finding bodies."

The waitress returned with two glasses of water, and a cup of coffee for me.

"Thank you," I said.

"I'm going to get this over with quick, Eddie," he said. "Maybe by the time my food comes you can leave and let me eat in peace."

"What's on your mind, Detective?"

He pointed his right index finger at me, probably the same one he'd poked me with. I noticed for the first time since meeting him how blunt it was, and that it was missing a nail. No, missing the entire tip.

"I got the word from above, Eddie, that I'm not supposed to press you for the name of your high roller," he explained, "but between you, me and the lamppost we know that Frank Sinatra sent you to find that girl."

"Is that right?"

"Yeah, that's right."

I stared at him, took a sip of my coffee.

"Is that all you came here to say, Detective?" I asked then.

"You're not going to admit it," he said, sitting back in his chair. "Hey, that's okay, you don't have to." He shrugged. "I just want you to tell that lounge singer something for me."

"Lounge singer?" I asked. "Why would you call one of our headliners, and a great actor to boot, a 'lounge singer,' Detective? You got something against him, too? Oh wait, don't tell me, let me guess. He's a mug too, isn't he? Because he works for the casino?"

"Don't kid yourself, Eddie," he said. "Sinatra's a bigger mug than you."

I sat back in my chair.

"I'll bet you got beat up a lot as a child," I said. "Bigger kids? Older? Probably Italian."

"What're you now, a shrink?"

"I'm just sayin' —"

"Well, stop saying," he snapped, cutting me off. "Tell Sinatra if he had anything to do with these murders I'll nail him."

"I'm sure he's heard that before," I said, and then added, "in the movies."

"You know something?" he said, throwing

his napkin down on the table. "Suddenly I don't have much of an appetite."

He stood up.

"Don't go away mad, Detective."

"I'll nail you, your big torpedo friend, and Sinatra," he said. "Remember that."

"Wait," I said, "that's if we had anything to do with the murders, right? Not just in general? I mean, I wanna get this straight."

"Fuck you, Eddie," he said, just as the girl appeared with his plate of food. He stalked off and she stared after him, then looked at me.

"Wha—" she said. "Hey, he didn't —"

"Don't worry about it," I said. "Wrap it up and I'll take it with me."

For Jerry.

FORTY-THREE

When I got back to the big guy he was doing exactly what I'd asked him to do, standing there with his arms folded across his chest, watching Barney Crane — who suddenly didn't look so arrogant. In fact, he looked downright uncomfortable.

"I brought you something," I said to Jerry, holding out the bag to him.

He looked at me, unfolded his arms and accepted the bag. He opened it and sniffed.

"Smells good," he said.

"Find someplace to sit and eat it."

"What happened with the cop?"

"He just wanted to warn me that you, me and Frank Sinatra were going down."

"Not a chance of him takin' Mr. S. down," he said.

"I wish you sounded as confident about you and me," I told him.

"Hey," he said, "we didn't do nothin'."

"I don't think that matters to the detective. Look, go sit in a corner and eat that and I'll come and find you."

"What about your buddy, there?" he asked, meaning Barney Crane.

"Give him one more long look before you go."

Jerry did that, then went and sat in front of a slot machine, digging eagerly into his doggy bag.

I looked over at Barney, who seemed even more perturbed. He waved me over.

"What's up, Barney?" I asked, innocently.

"What's with your boy there, Eddie?" he asked.

"My boy?"

"Your pet torpedo."

"He doesn't like to be called that."

"Well then, whatever he is, does he have a problem with me?"

Physically, Barney was a lightweight. I mean, really, if he was a fighter he'd be a lightweight — a tall one. He had height, but he had no meat on his bones.

"Whataya mean?"

"He's been starin' at me for the past half hour," Barney said. "And I mean . . . glarin' at me, you know? Like I fucked his sister or something."

"Well, he doesn't have a sister," I said. "All I can tell you is that he says he likes blackjack, and can spot a cheater a mile away."

"A cheater?"

"That's what he said."

"I ain't seen him play a hand."

"Oh, he doesn't play anymore."

"Why not?"

"He says he killed the last guy he caught cheating," I explained. "Ever since then he doesn't play. Now he just watches . . . and waits."

"Waits? For what?"

"For the next cheater."

Barney swallowed.

"I, uh, don't have no cheaters at my table, Eddie," he said. "You know that."

"Well, then that's good, Barney," I said. "That's real good. You keep it that way."

I walked over to where Jerry had already polished off his sandwich. He was licking brown gravy from his fingertips.

"What're we pullin' on him?" he asked.

"I'll tell you later," I said.

He balled up the bag and dropped it into a garbage bin.

"Where we goin' now?"

"Back to my house," I said. "If you're sure there's not a hit out on me I guess we'll be safe there."

"I'm tellin' ya, Mr. G.," he said. "There's

no hit on ya."

"Okay, then," I said. "You drive."

We were heading for the back door when I spotted something and stopped short.

"What?" Jerry asked, almost running into me.

"See that girl over there? The one tapping her foot at the blackjack table?"

"Like she's sittin' on an anthill or somethin'?" he asked.

"That's the one."

"She's a looker."

"Yeah," I said, "but she's also Mary Clarke's sister, Lily."

"I thought she went upstairs to her room with yer buddy Bardini?"

"I guess they didn't stay up there."

"She tell you she came here to gamble?"

"No," I said, "she just said she had to come to try to help her sister."

"But gamble in the meantime, huh?"

"I didn't get that impression," I said. "In fact, I had the distinct impression she'd never been to Vegas before."

"Maybe she's a beginner."

"I don't think so."

"Why not?"

"That's not a low-limit table."

FORTY-FOUR

We stood and watched for fifteen minutes. During that time she lost over five thousand dollars, and I had no idea how long she'd been sitting there and how much she'd lost before we arrived.

"Somethin's hinky, huh?" Jerry asked.

"Very hinky," I said, "except . . ."

"Except what?"

"She told me she works as a bookkeeper."

"Are you thinkin' she's playin' with somebody else's money?"

"If that's true," I said, "then I really am not the judge of character I thought I was."

"Or," Jerry offered, "she's just really good."

"I would prefer it that way," I said.

As we watched she made a huge bet, took two hits and busted. I couldn't see what she'd been hitting on, but my keen instincts told me she should have stood.

"Jerry," I said, "I need you to make a

phone call, and I need you to say exactly what I tell you to say."

"No problem, Mr. G."

Fifteen minutes later an annoyed-looking Frank Sinatra came into the casino wearing a raincoat with the collar turned up. He attracted some attention, but not for the reason he usually would.

He spotted Jerry and me and came walking over.

"You wanna tell me why I'm wearin' a raincoat in the middle of the desert?" he asked.

Maybe I should have asked him why he had brought a raincoat to the middle of the desert, but I decided against it.

"Frank," I said, "have you ever met Lily D'Angeli?"

"Lily — who the hell . . . wait a minute. You talkin' about Mary's sister?"

"That's right. Did you ever meet her?"

"Well, not exactly . . . I saw her in the Ambassador one night, talking to Mary."

"But you never met."

"I just said that, Eddie," he snapped.

"Okay, I'm sorry," I said. "I'm just trying to be sure."

"I'm sure."

"Okay, then look over there at the center

blackjack table and tell me who you see?"

He looked, then looked again.

"That's Lily . . . I think."

"You think?"

"Well . . . she looks an awful lot like Mary with brown hair."

"Frank . . . could that be Mary?"

"Why would Mary —"

"Could it be her?" I prodded.

He looked again, then said, "I've got to get closer."

"Okay, but I don't want to spook her."

There was no need to worry. Even though people were looking at us — and some of them even recognized Frank, finally — Lily D'Angeli was so intent on her cards that she never looked up.

When he'd gotten a good enough look we withdrew again. In fact, I pulled him behind some slot machines. Jerry got the picture then and gave us some extra shelter by using his bulk.

"Frank?"

"It's not Mary," he said. "It looks a lot like her, but it ain't."

"Okay."

"So if that's her sister, Lily, what the hell is she doin' here?"

I told him that after I spoke to her on the phone she decided to hop a plane to Vegas to see if she could find her sister.

"Then why is she playing blackjack?" he asked. "And at a high-limit table?"

"That's what I intend to find out," I said. "Did Mary ever tell you anything about Lily?"

"Like what?"

"Her job, whether or not she gambled . . ."

"Mary told me her sister was a prude, didn't like to have fun and didn't want Mary to have fun."

"And her job."

"I dunno — wait." He stroked the corners of his mouth with thumb and forefinger. "I think she said once that she was a book-keeper. I remember because Mary said she couldn't imagine a more boring job, so it was perfect for her sister."

"Okay," I said, "okay."

"Maybe I should go and talk to this chick," Frank suggested.

"Well, one of the other things she told me was that she didn't like you," I said. "If that's true she won't talk to you."

"How could she not like me?" he demanded. "We've never met."

"Apparently, she thinks you're a bad influence on her sister."

"What about her? She's betting money by

the bucket up there. What kind of influence is she?"

"That's what I'm going to find out," I said. "It's time for me and sister Lily to have another talk."

I had Jerry walk Frank to the elevator, to make sure he got there safe. I also didn't want him changing his mind about talking to Lily.

While Jerry was gone I went to the front desk to check and see if Lily had deposited anything in the hotel safe — like a chunk of money. She was pulling it out of her purse by the bundle, so she had to have more of it somewhere. The word I got from the desk, though, was that she hadn't deposited a thing.

I asked for the head of security before going to find Jerry again. I needed a favor, and by dropping Entratter's name I got it.

I intercepted Jerry before he could reenter the casino.

"I'm gonna get you into Lily D'Angeli's room," I said. "I want you to search it while I keep her busy."

"What am I lookin' for?"

"Anything," I said. "Money, anything writ-

256

ten down, like an address or phone number."

"Okay."

I handed him a key I'd gotten from security, with the promise that I'd return it within the hour. It took a lot of talking for me to convince them that they didn't have to go to the room with Jerry.

I grabbed Jerry's arm before he could get away.

"This needs to be done neatly, Jerry."

"Neatly?" He frowned.

"By that I mean don't toss the room," I said. "I don't want her to know it's been searched. Can you do that?"

"I can be neat," he promised.

"Okay, then," I said. "I'll see you down here in a while. Try to be quick about it, I don't know how long I'll be able to hold her."

"I got faith in you, Mr. G."

"I've got faith in you, too, Jerry."

Forty-Five

I went back to the blackjack tables and Lily was still there. In fact, she was now the only player at that table. I caught the eye of the pit boss. It was John Kelly, the guy who had asked me about raising the table limit for Vic Damone.

"John, how long has she been playing?" I asked.

"About an hour."

"How much has she lost?"

"Ten grand, I guess," he said. "She started out winning, was up about that much. Is somethin' wrong with this twist? She's playing cash. Keeps diggin' it out of her purse."

"No, nothing's wrong, but I'm gonna have to take her off the table for a while. I have to talk to her."

"That's Jake with me, Eddie. She's about due to start winnin' again, anyway."

"Go back to work and don't worry."

"I ain't worried," he said. "She's a looker,

though. You got a beef with her —"

"I'm workin' here, John," I said. "Jack wants me to check her out."

At the mention of Entratter's name his eyes widened. John Kelly was the youngest pit boss in the Sands and even though it was Jack himself who promoted him, Kelly was afraid of him.

"Oh, okay, I see," he stammered. "I'll, uh, go back to work."

"Good idea."

I waited for him to retake his position in the pit, and then moved up behind Lily. This was the first time I was close enough to see her cards. She had fifteen and asked for a hit. The dealer gave her a seven, so she busted at twenty-two.

"You should always stay on fifteen," I said.

"Fuck off," she said, "I've got a system."

I sidled up next to her and said, "It doesn't look like a very good one."

"Hey, who the hell —" she started, but when she turned her head and saw me her mouth snapped shut.

"Why do I get the feelin' you're not the demure sister I thought you were?"

I could see her brain working behind her eyes. Stay with her story or admit she'd been found out and try something new?

"Look," she finally said, "my sister doesn't

know I gamble. It's not something I'm proud of."

"Well taking a hit on fifteen," I said, "I wouldn't think so."

"Eddie —"

"Cash in your chips, Lily," I said. "we're going to have another talk."

The only place to take somebody to have a private talk in the Sands would be an office off the casino floor. But I didn't have an office and at that moment I didn't want to take the time to try to borrow one. That left the lounge or the coffee shop, which is where I usually ended up with somebody like Jerry, or Joey Bishop, or even Entratter himself. But I didn't want to go into the lounge with Lily in case Bev was there, and I'd just recently been in the coffee shop with Hargrove, the cop.

So I said to Lily D'Angeli, "Let's go for a walk."

She cashed out her chips, shoved the money into her purse, then stepped down off her stool, clutching the bag to her.

"I'm not gonna steal your bag," I said. "Between the two of us, I'm the one tellin' the truth about what I'm doing."

"Look, I —"

"Save it for outside," I said, taking her by

260

the arm.

"I could scream, you know," she threatened, taking quick steps to keep up as I headed for the door.

"Go ahead," I said. "This is my casino, remember?"

She closed her mouth and came along a lot easier.

Once we were outside on the street I released her arm. She rubbed it, as if I'd hurt her, but the guilt act wasn't going to work with me.

"Is it safe to be out here at night?" she asked.

"Safe," I said, "and pretty. Look at all the lights."

"What's that over there, all lit up?"

I knew what she meant without turning my head.

"That's the Flamingo."

"Bugsy Siegel's place?" Her eyes widened.

"That's right."

"Can we get a drink in Bugsy's Bar?" she asked.

"Sure, why not."

We started walking toward the Flamingo. She stared at the famous names on the marquees — Nat King Cole, Keeley Smith — with big eyes. She was wearing glasses, maybe because she needed them to see the cards better. She hadn't been wearing them the first time we met. She was beautiful, whether it was the neon lighting her, or the moon.

"You're staring," she said, then suddenly grabbed the glasses and went, "Oh."

"Leave them on, if you need them," I said. "They look good."

"Mary always said — oh, never mind." But she put them back on. The lenses gave her only a slightly myopic look. The frames were made of plastic and were hardly noticeable.

"What's going on, Lily?" I asked.

"What do you mean?"

"Supposedly you came here to help your sister, not to gamble."

"I got bored in my room," she said. "I was only doing it to pass the time."

"Thirty grand to pass the time?"

She firmed her chin.

"It's my money. I saved it. I can do what I want with it."

"That's very true."

While lots of places and people involved with Vegas have gotten a bad rap over the years, the Flamingo and Bugsy Siegel were not among them. Sure, it cost Bugsy six million instead of two to build it, and it was a flop when he opened, and eventually the mob had him killed and replaced him with someone who made it a success, but to most people Benny Siegel is still seen as the man who "discovered" Las Vegas. The Flamingo is still perceived as the "first" Las Vegas casino. Neither of those things is true. Herb McDonald's El Rancho Vegas predates the Flamingo, as does The Frontier. But more than that, Bugsy did not even break ground on what soon became the Flamingo. It had already been started by the time he came on the scene. About the only thing Bugsy could take real credit for was the name "Flamingo," which was a nickname he gave Virginia Hill. And even then the place had been renamed The "Fabulous" Flamingo in 1952.

But to certain parties it would always be Bugsy's Place.

Bugsy's Bar was right in the center of the casino on a raised floor. It was a Wednesday night and even in a town that never sleeps some nights are better than others to do certain things. Midweek was still the best time to be in a bar at night. Like most towns Friday and Saturday were the busiest, but on this night we were able to get two stools at the bar together, and the noise decibel would not keep us from hearing each other speak.

I realized while we were waiting for the bartender to bring our drinks — beer for me and a Manhattan for the lady — that I had apparently taken Jerry's assurance to heart that there was no hit out on me. Why else would I have left the Sands without him? Suddenly, I looked at the men around us to see if anyone was paying attention to us. They were, but it was only because of Lily.

When the bartender brought our drinks she grabbed hers like a drowning woman. She held it with both hands and gulped.

"Lily, suppose you start by telling me why you really came to Vegas?" I said.

"I told you," she said. "To see if I could help my sister."

"That wasn't on the level, Lily."

"It was," she said. "The part that wasn't on the level was me being, uh, sort of —"

"A prude?"

"Well, yeah . . ."

"Why'd you tell me that?"

"Because it's worked on men before."

"So you and your sister aren't so different?"

"Let's just say we're a lot more alike than I let on," she said. "But Mary's always been more, um, obvious than I have."

"Like the blond hair?"

264

"Right."

"So what do you really do for a living?"

"Oh, that part was true," she said. "I really am a bookkeeper."

"Lily," I asked, "do you know where Mary is?"

"No, I don't. Really."

"And you really did send her some money?"

"You know I did," she said. "You found the Western Union office I sent it to."

That was true.

"I told her I'd come and meet her but she said no, just send the money."

"But you came, anyway."

"Yes."

"And you brought some money with you for her?"

"Right."

"And a whole bunch to gamble with."

She bit her lip.

"And it's not yours?"

She finished her drink and put the empty glass on the bar. The barman must have been watching her because he set another down within seconds.

"I wanted to bring Mary enough to do her some good."

"So you . . . borrowed it?"

"I thought I could come here, use my

265

system and replace the money when I got home."

"You really do have a system?"

"Of course."

"That calls for you to hit on fifteen?"

She gave me a dirty look.

"It's a system, it takes time to work."

"Lily . . . you embezzled money from your employer to gamble with?"

"Well," she said with a shrug, "I borrowed it from my boss."

"Without him knowing it?"

"Kinda."

"What happens when he realizes it's gone," I said. "Won't he call the police?"

"No."

"Why not?"

"He can't."

"Why not?" I asked, and then it dawned on me. "Jesus, he's not mobbed up, is he? A mob accountant?"

"No, no, of course not," she said.

"Then what —"

"He, uh . . ."

"Just spit it out, Lily."

"Fine," she said. "He kinda stole it himself."

FORTY-SIX

"Okay," I said, "let me get this straight — your boss is the embezzler?"

"Right."

"And you stole the money from him."

"Borrowed," she said. "I'm going to give it back when I get home."

"Isn't he wondering where it is right now?" I asked.

"Maybe," she said, "but he can't go to the cops, and he can't tell his wife —"

"His wife?"

She nodded. "He'd have to tell her we've been sleeping together."

"You've been sleeping with your boss, the embezzler? And you borrowed money from him that he stole. And I was supposed to believe that of the two sisters you were the prude?"

"Well," she said, looking at me demurely above her drink, "I told you that was a lie."

"And that was the only lie?"

"Yes," she said. "I'm really here to try to help Mary."

"And make some money gambling in the meanwhile."

"It was an opportunity I had to take," she explained. "Roger will understand. Who knows when I'd get the chance to come to Vegas again?"

"Roger?"

"My boss. Roger —"

I held up my hand and said, "I don't need to know his name." Whoever stole the money — her boss, her — I didn't need to get involved in that. She could deal with the consequences of that when she got back home.

"Look," she said, "I'm sorry I played the poor-little-pitiful-me card on you and your handsome friend."

"Danny," I said. "What happened to him?"

"When I wouldn't let him in my room to comfort me he said he had to go."

"You didn't let him in?"

"Well, I might have," she said, "but I wanted to get to the blackjack table."

"Why would you choose to play in the Sands," I asked, "where I might see you?"

"You told me you weren't working your regular job," she said. "I didn't think you'd be around. And besides, I really don't have to explain myself to you. If I want to play blackjack I can."

"You're right," I said. "If you want to sleep with your boss, and steal money that he already stole, come to Vegas and gamble it, that's your business."

"Thank you."

"Um," I said, "how much did you . . . borrow?"

She stared at me. "You're not going to turn me in?"

"No," I said. "I've got other fish to fry, Lily. I'm just . . . curious."

She hesitated, then said, "Fifty thousand."

"Fifty — ?" I stopped and lowered my voice. "Fifty thousand?"

"That's right."

"You don't have it all in your purse right now, do you?"

"No."

"It's in your room?"

"Well, yes," she said. "I did hide it, but your maids wouldn't steal, would they?"

"Hell," I said, "every chance they get. Come on." I tossed some money on the bar.

"Where?"

"We're gonna get that money into a safe," I said. "You can withdraw it whenever you want to play."

"B-but . . . it's stolen," she whispered.

"Nobody knows that but you and me."

We were on our way up in the elevator before I realized what the heck I was doing. Jerry could have still been searching her room and I was bringing her up there myself. I checked my watch. If he did it the way we had planned, he'd be gone by now.

And he was. The room was empty and — from what I could see — didn't look as if it had been tossed. It smelled heavily of her perfume. I tried to remember if Jerry wore aftershave or cologne, but there wasn't a hint of either in the air. The room looked kind of messy, but she had freshened up and changed her clothes — a similar suit in a different color — and I assumed the mess was hers.

"Okay," I said, "let's get the money and take it downstairs."

Suddenly, she stopped and turned to look at me. I could read her face. She was alone in her room with a man she barely knew, and most of fifty thousand dollars.

"Lily," I said, "I'm not going to steal your money."

"How do I know that?" she asked. "You know that it's already stolen. You could take it and I couldn't do a thing."

I waggled my index finger at her and said,

"Now you're trying to talk me into it."

She studied me for a moment, then said, "Okay, I'm going to trust you."

"Good."

She turned to get the money, then turned back.

"Isn't this what high rollers do?"

"What?"

"Put their money in the hotel safe."

"Some do."

"So I'm a high roller?"

"Technically."

"Then shouldn't I have a bigger room?"

I had put her in a standard, one big bed, a chest of drawers, a chair, a table and a TV

"This'll do," I said. "Let's not push it. Remember, we both know where the money came from."

"Right," she said. "No harm in asking."

She had loosened up quite a bit — in part, probably, because of the two drinks. When she wasn't playing the prudish sister she was beautiful and sexy, without even trying to be. I suddenly became the one aware of how alone we were. There I was with a gorgeous, sweet-smelling girl and fifty thousand dollars. The girl or the money would have been a big temptation to most men. But both . . .

I shook my head. I may have been a lot of

things, but a thief wasn't one of them, not even if — technically speaking — I was employed by the mob.

She pulled a bundle wrapped in brown paper from beneath the bed, bending over and giving me a good look at her ass and garters.

"Where was that when we met?" I asked.

"In my suitcase."

"Okay," I said, "let's go."

"Should we count it?"

"They do that downstairs," I answered, "and give you a receipt."

"And a line of credit in the casino?" she asked.

I hesitated, then said, "Sure, why not?"

As we went back down in the elevator I figured, stolen or not, why shouldn't the Sands have a shot at all that cash?

FORTY-SEVEN

When I woke up the next morning in Lily's room, in her bed, with her, naked, it took me a while to reconstruct the events that had brought me there.

We'd gone downstairs to put her money in the hotel safe. Then I arranged for her to have a modest line of credit, one that would at least keep her from blowing the whole wad in one day. After that we went to the lounge for another drink. Bev was there. She and Lily immediately stared daggers at each other. At that point Lily became amorous. We had a couple more drinks and I didn't mind her draping herself all over me. It not only got the attention of Beverly, but of all the other men in the place. Lily was, after all, beautiful. She had the smoothest skin, which I discovered when she allowed me to stroke her thigh. Up close her perfume had an even headier scent — or maybe that was the booze, talking. I had graduated from beer to bourbon at some point. Maybe I was looking for an excuse to loosen up and Lily coming on to me was just the ticket — even if she was doing it to get Bev's goat.

The rest is kind of a blur, though I do remember staggering into her room and pulling each other's clothes off. By that time it was no longer an act, we wanted each other and we went at it like — well, a couple of drunks. She scratched me, I bit her too hard on the breast — although I plead guilty to the fact that they were eminently bitable, and so I had no choice. I think we even bumped heads once, but then I remember attaining a sweet, matched rhythm that took us both where we wanted to go.

I turned over and looked down at her. She was on her back, the sheet down to her waist. Her breasts were amazing, pale, smooth, firm and full; her whole body had a lushness her clothes were somehow able to disguise. My first hint had been when I'd put my hand on her thigh and found it not only smooth, but firm.

I found myself wanting to lean down and kiss each pink nipple, but stopped myself because the whole night had been a mistake. We weren't lovers waking in each other's arms, eager to go at it again. We were two people who had gotten drunk and fallen into bed together.

I was also afraid that if I woke her she'd scream.

I pulled the sheet back and swung my feet to the floor. The clock next to the bed said it was 8:00 a.m. But before I could get up I felt her hand on my back.

"Where are you goin'?" she asked, sleepily.

I looked over my shoulder at her. Her eyes were open — bleary, but open.

"I thought I should, uh, go," I said, lamely.

She licked her lips and asked, "Why?" Her mouth, now moist, was possibly the most erotic thing I'd seen in a while — and I'd just spent the night exploring her whole body.

"Well, I thought you might, uh, I mean, I thought maybe —"

"We made a mistake?"

"Well . . . yeah."

"I didn't," she said, smiling. "I wanted to lay you. Did you make a mistake?"

"Well . . . I was drunk. . . ."

She stroked my back, her finger lingering right at the crack of my ass.

"It sure didn't feel like a mistake," she said, and then stretched, her breasts going taut. "But if you want to go . . . go."

"And if I want to stay?"

"Then get over here, big boy," she said. "I'm not done with you, yet."

I got downstairs at about ten-thirty, partly because I'd stopped off at my locker for some fresh clothes. When I hit the casino floor I was almost assaulted by Jerry.

"Where the fuck you been, Mr. G.?" Outrage, tinged with respect. He really was an amazing guy.

"I'm sorry, Jerry —"

"I searched the broad's room like you said, and then you disappeared."

"You been worried about me, Jerry?"

"Damn right I been worried," he said. "Somethin' happens ta you I get in a lot of trouble, ya know?"

"That the only reason?"

He studied me for a moment, then took a step back.

"You got laid last night," he said, suddenly. "You sonofabitch." He sniffed the air. "Drunk and laid."

I grabbed his arm and said, "Come 'ere," and pulled him over to a closed blackjack table, where we each took a seat.

"It was a mistake," I said. "we both got drunk and —"

"And she's a looker," he said. "Great tits,

I bet, huh?"

He had such an eager look on his face I couldn't bear to disappoint him.

"Yeah, Jerry, great tits."

"I knew it!"

"What did you find in her room?"

"Nothin'," he said, "and I looked good — and I was neat. I mean, she was kinda messy, but I left the room the way I found it."

"I know," I said. "I saw it. You did a good job, but there was nothing there?"

"Well . . ."

"Well what?"

"I found a bundle of money under the bed," he said. "Wrapped in brown paper."

"Jerry . . ."

"I didn't take any," he said. "I ain't no thief. I coulda, but I didn't."

"Good," I said. Actually, I remember now that when we counted it at the front desk the amount had not surprised her. We had put forty-two thousand in the vault.

"So what happened?" he asked. "Did you get anything out of her — I mean, besides fuckin' her?"

I told him about the conversation I had with Lily and he started to laugh.

"What's so funny?"

"Everybody's always complainin' about

the mob," he said, chuckling. "Here's a guy stealin' from his boss, and a girl stealin' from her boss, who she's fuckin' — who's married! Ain't it funny? How come that kinda crime don't make the papers?"

"You're right," I said, "and I don't know the answer to that one."

"So where does this leave us, Mr G.?"

"It leaves us with the premier tonight, and still no Mary Clarke," I said.

"Maybe she'll show up there."

"If she'd show up there, why not come here? We could put her in a room and protect her."

"For how long?" he asked. "That wouldn't tell ya who's tryin' ta kill 'er, or why. You gotta find that out before she can be safe."

"You've got a point there," I said.

"And what about the dead guys?" he asked. "Not countin' the one I killed. Who killed them?"

"That's Hargrove's job."

"What if it was her?" he asked. "You gonna protect her then?"

"I guess that'd be up to Frank," I said.

"You mean if you knew she killed them guys you wouldn't turn her in?"

Suddenly, I didn't want to disappoint Jerry with my answer.

"Jerry," I said, "I guess that would depend

278

on why she killed them."

He gave me a light punch on the shoulder — light for him or I'd still be sporting a bruise from it — and said, "Like I always say, Mr. G. You're a stand-up guy."

FORTY-EIGHT

Jack Entratter looked up at me as I approached his desk.

"You look like hell."

And despite having had sex the night before — and that morning — with a beautiful woman, I did feel like hell. It was only after I finally left Lily's bed — with the promise to call her later — that I realized what a hangover I had.

"Some aspirin would help," I said, dropping myself into a chair.

He used the intercom to tell his girl to bring some in. She handed them to me with a glass of water and I said, "Thanks," gratefully. She gave me a disapproving look and left.

"What's on your mind, kid?"

I told him about Mary Clarke's sister coming to Vegas and about putting her in a room. I didn't bother telling him where I spent last night.

"What's she doin' here?"

"Looking for her sister," I said, "but she also brought a bundle to play blackjack with."

"God, maybe we'll make somethin' from this deal, after all. What else?"

"I gotta ask, did you put the screws to Hargrove so he wouldn't ask about Frank?"

"Not me. Why?"

"He said he got the word not to ask."

"I don't have that kind of pull with the Police Department," he said. "Now the Sheriff's Department, that'd be another story."

"Could Frank pull something like that off on his own?" I asked.

"I doubt it."

"Then who —"

I stopped short and we both looked at each other.

"MoMo," I said.

Entratter shrugged. "He's in town, ain't he?"

"Why would he stick his neck out like that?"

"He likes Frank."

"I know they're friends, but —"

"I didn't say they was friends," he corrected me. "I think even if you asked Frank that question he'd say they weren't."

"Then what are they?"

Entratter sat back in his chair.

"I think they both just like having the other one's phone number, you know?"

"Well, whatever the reason," I said, "if MoMo's protecting Frank, that looks bad for him."

Entratter spread his hands.

"Who's gonna tell him that?"

"Maybe I will."

"That I'd like to see, kid," he said. "You got anything more for me? I got work to do."

"The premier's tonight," I said.

"You're tellin' me somethin' I already know."

"Did you send your man back to the Western Union office this morning?"

"I sent a man," he said. "Not the same one, but with the same orders. She ain't gonna show up, is she?"

"No."

He spread his hands, as if to say, we're done, but when I got to the door he called out, "Work the sister, kid. I'll bet she knows more than she's telling."

"You're probably right, Jack," I said. "Thanks for the advice."

I had a bad feeling. Jerry was good to talk

to, but the guy I needed right now was Danny.

When I got back to the main floor I went straight to a phone and called his office. Luckily, I found him in and he agreed to meet me.

"You want off the strip?" he asked.

"That doesn't matter."

"How about the D.I.? I gotta see a guy over there."

"Desert Inn it is," I said.

"Half an hour?"

"You're the best, Danny."

"Bring the Gunsel."

"He wouldn't miss it."

I found Jerry and told him we were going to see Danny at the Desert Inn.

"He got somethin' for us?"

"I just have to talk to him," I answered.

"We drivin'?"

We could have walked, but I wanted to have the car with us so I said, "Yeah, we're drivin'."

When it came to driving the Caddy Jerry was like a big kid and I didn't have the heart to take the keys away from him.

FORTY-NINE

The Desert Inn was built in 1950, the first Vegas strip hotel to come up with the idea of using dancing waters as an attraction. Wilbur Clark also moved away from the 1940's-style rectangular swimming pool in the back that the El Rancho, Last Frontier, Flamingo and the Thunderbird still had and went with a more curved, modern shape. The D.I. was Clark's attempt to bring Palm Springs to the desert.

We parked out back but walked around to come in the front. We paused long enough for Jerry to stare at the fountain.

The D.I. lounge was glass-enclosed on three sides and resembled an airport tower. It offered a very clear view of the desert. Danny and I had arranged to meet there, but we weren't going in.

"Let's go to the pool," I said. "We can get a drink there."

Jerry seemed disappointed at not being

able to go into the lounge, but he followed Danny and me outside.

The view around the pool was spectacular. It didn't matter if the women were wearing one-piece bathing suits or bikinis, they were all gorgeous. We found three chaise lounges, ordered drinks and sat down. Danny took off his sports jacket and laid it over the back of his chair. Jerry couldn't do it because of his shoulder holster. I was wearing a shirt and no jacket and a pair of jeans, my backup clothes from my locker.

"Not used to seein' you look so casual, pal," Danny said to me. "And look at the Gunsel, sweatin' in his jacket."

"Jerry, when your drink comes you can take it inside," I told him. "No use you roasting out here."

And the August heat would have done just that to him. When the waiter came with our drinks Jerry said, "I'll be just inside, where I can still see you."

"He takes his responsibility very seriously, doesn't he?"

"That he does."

"So if I, say, tried to throw you into the pool he'd come runnin' out?"

"Probably not," I said, "but if you tried to shoot me he'd be here."

"I left my rod in my office." He took a

drink and loosened his shirt and tie. "What's on your mind? I like the heat, but I'm not dressed for it."

"Wanna go to the lounge?"

A girl in a bikini walked by, her peach-sized breasts barely confined, and he said, "You're kiddin', right?"

"Okay," I said. "I think maybe I'm being played."

He had to tear his eyes from the girl's twitching butt.

"By who?"

"That's a good question."

"And why?"

"Another one."

"Okay, let's try this," he said. "What makes you think you're bein' played?"

"Nothing seems right," I said. "Somebody's keeping the cops from asking about Frank, and it's not Entratter."

"Who then?"

"I'm thinkin' Giancana."

"If he was gonna do that, why not just have some of his men find the girl?"

"Maybe he is," I said. "Maybe he's lyin' about not caring about Frank and Mary."

"So he sends somebody to kill her?" Danny asked. "And protects Frank from the cops?"

"The way I get it, MoMo likes having a

286

movie star in his circle."

"And Frank?"

"He likes havin' a pet mobster."

"You really think he thinks Giancana's his pet?"

"I don't know," I said. "I like Frank, but he thinks JFK is his great friend. Maybe he actually thinks MoMo is his friend, too."

"So who else you think is playin' you?"

"How about the girl?"

"Mary?"

I shook my head.

"Lily."

"Her? The prudish one?"

"Turns out she's not."

"She wouldn't let me in her room."

"Well . . ."

He turned his head sharply. "You didn't."

I opened my mouth to respond, but he cut me off.

"You did, didn't you? You sonofabitch! How'd you do it?"

I explained it to him, from finding her at the blackjack table to the drunken coupling in her room, and the morning after.

"Wow," he said, shaking his head. "She was good. She had me fooled."

"Me, too," I said, "and if she's that good, who's to say she doesn't still have me fooled?"

"You think she's involved, somehow?"

"Somebody's doin' somethin', Danny," I said. "I mean . . . somebody's got to be pullin' the strings here."

"Who gets your vote?"

"Giancana," I said. "I mean, he's the one with the power. But maybe the sister . . ." I shook my head.

"I can run a check on her, Eddie," he said. "I'll make some calls and get back to you. But don't overlook the possibility that it's the other sister pullin' the strings."

"Okay, Danny, I appreciate it," I said. "If I could get some money out of this for you —"

"Forget it." Another woman went by, this one with a Jayne Mansfield figure packed into a one-piece suit cut low in front and back. We both watched until she was out of sight.

"I can't do a thing about MoMo, though," he went on. "That's got to be up to you."

"I know."

"Sorry I'm not much help."

"I just needed to say some of this stuff out loud, Danny."

"You couldn't have said it to Jerry?"

"Yeah, but you're my pet P.I."

He was about to say something when a gorgeous Negro girl went by in some kind of Brazilian suit, her body gleaming in the sunlight, not an ounce of fat on her.

"Okay," he said, "I've had enough sun and cock-teasin' for one day."

We both gulped down the rest of our drinks, although I didn't really taste mine and couldn't tell you today what it was.

Jerry was holding a half-finished beer when we reached him.

"A lot of pretty broads out there," he said, staring out the window.

"Jerry, my boy," Danny said, slapping him on his broad back, "go to any pool in any hotel in Vegas and you'll find the most beautiful women in the world just waitin' for you."

"For you, maybe," Jerry said.

"Don't sell yourself short, Gunsel," Danny said. "Lots of women like big, brawny men."

Jerry looked around for a surface to put his bottle down on and chose a windowsill.

"We goin'?" he asked me.

"Yep, we're goin'."

The three of us walked through the D.I. to the front door and stepped outside together.

"I'll call you," Danny promised me. "So long, Gunsel. Keep our boy safe."

"That's my job, dick."

Danny laughed and went back inside. It

was then I remembered he said he had to see somebody at the Desert Inn.

"That guy gets lots of broads, huh?"

"Plenty."

Jerry looked at me and grinned.

"But you got the girl last night, huh?" he said. "You tell 'im?"

I couldn't help but grin back.

"He dragged it out of me."

FIFTY

When we got in the Caddy, Jerry started the motor and asked, "Where to?"

I was momentarily stumped.

"Mr. G.?"

"I'm thinking, Jerry."

"It's hot," he said. "Can we go someplace where you can think inside? Why's it always so hot here?"

"If you'd take your jacket off you wouldn't be so hot."

"I'm packin' my piece."

"I know."

He sat quietly while the motor purred.

"Car's runnin' great," he said.

"I've got a guy who takes good care of it."

"You don't do it yourself?"

"No," I said. "I can change the oil and replace spark plugs, but that's about it."

"Man, a car like this you gotta take care of it yerself." He caressed the steering wheel.

"Yeah, well, maybe I'll learn."

"You sure your guy is good?"

"Listen to the engine."

"I got a guy in Brooklyn," he said, "he's the best. I'll bet he could recommend somebody —"

"I told you, Jerry, I've got a guy."

But he dug into his pocket anyway for his guy's address and phone number, and as he pulled his hand out something fell onto the seat between us.

"What's this?" I picked it up. It looked like a plane ticket stub. "Is this yours?"

"Aw, hell, I forgot," he said. "I picked that up off the floor in your girl's room. It's just the stub, it ain't her return ticket, or nothin'."

Plane tickets are issued with several copies, and although this looked like the bottom copy and was faint, I could read her name, her flight number, the time and the date of her flight.

The date . . .

"Jerry, you picked this up off the floor of her room?" I asked.

"That's right."

"Why?"

"It was next to the wastebasket. I figured she threw it out, and I just stuck it in my pocket. I didn't find nothin' else, Mr. G. I figured I might as well take somethin'. Why, is it important?"

"Important?" I asked. "Jerry, I think this is the piece of the puzzle."

"What puzzle?"

"The puzzle that will tell us who's been jerkin' who around."

"Mr. G., you're talkin' too fast."

"According to this ticket stub Miss Lily D'Angeli flew into Vegas on the same day her sister checked into the Golden Nugget."

"I still don't —"

"She told us she got here yesterday," I said. "According to this she's been in Vegas for days."

"Well . . . I guess that is important."

"Let's get back to the Sands, Jerry," I said, "and we'll find out just how important."

He put the car in drive and said, "But Mr. G. —"

"Yeah?"

"Didn't you talk to her on the phone in Chicago?" he asked. "How could you've done that if she was here?"

I closed my eyes and pressed the ticket stub to my forehead, as if the answer would come to me that way.

"Jerry," I said, "my friend, I keep tellin' you you're smarter than you think."

FIFTY-ONE

Despite the fact that Jerry made a very good point I was sure we had found something that would help clear this mess up. I had a feeling these sisters were working some kind of a scam, only I couldn't think what it might be. And just who were they scamming?

We parked in the back of the Sands again and hurried inside. I didn't know why I was running, I just felt a sense of urgency.

As we headed for the elevator the concierge cut us off.

"Eddie, I've been lookin' for you."

"Why?"

"Your girl," he said. "She's gone."

"Gone?"

"Took her money out of the safe and left."

"Fuck!" I snapped.

"Wha—"

"When did she leave?"

"About an hour ago. The front desk told

me to find you. I guess they didn't want to give her the money without you, but when I couldn't locate you they had to. I mean . . . it was hers, right?"

"Sort of."

"Sort of. Wha—"

"Forget it, Charlie," I said. "Thanks for the heads up."

"Sure."

I turned to Jerry and again said, "Fuck. Now we've got to find both sisters."

"Both of 'em?"

"They're playin' us, Jerry. I don't know how or why, but they are. Look, you've got to do something for me. I have to get back to the D.I. before Danny leaves. There's something else I've got to ask him."

"But I gotta come with you —"

"No, you have to check on Frank."

"Mr. S.?"

"I want to make sure he's okay. I don't know why Lily came here, and I don't know why she left so quickly, but I want to make sure she didn't get to Frank."

"Mr. G., if somethin' happens ta you —"

"Nothing's going to happen," I said. "I promise. In fact, I'll call the D.I. and try to catch Danny."

"Okay, then —"

"Go," I said. "I'll be here in the lobby

when you get back."

He ran for the elevators. I went to a house phone and got an outside line to the D.I. Once connected I asked them to page Danny Bardini, while I waited on the line. I was still waiting when Jerry came back.

"We may have to go and find Danny," I said. "How's Frank?"

"George said he's at the theater for a final run-through," Jerry said. "Him and Mr. Martin, and Sammy and —"

"Hello? Danny?"

"What the hell?" Danny's voice came over the line. "Didn't we just —"

"Listen, Danny, the girl's gone. She got her money and took off."

"What the fuck," he said. "Now you've got to find both of them."

"I know, but I need you to do something else for me. The girl said she's a bookkeeper in Chicago. I want you to find out who for. Who her boss is."

"You don't want much. All we've got is a name — and maybe that's not real."

"I think it is. I've got it on an airline ticket stub."

"That doesn't mean —"

"I know, I know, but it's all we've got." I explained to him about the date on the stub.

"Okay, they're playin' some kinda game,"

he said. "I'll call the other hotels and see if she ever checked in to any of them. What the hell was she playin' at comin' to the Sands to find you?"

"I don't know," I said. "I guess I'll ask when we find her."

"And her sister," Danny said. "I'm givin' this my full attention now, Eddie."

"Thanks, Danny."

I hung up and looked at Jerry.

"Now what?"

"Let's get down to Fremont Street," I said. "I still want to check on Frank."

"Will we get in if we don't call ahead?" he asked as we headed for the car.

"Let's hope the same guys are still at the door when we get there."

The same guys were not at the door when we got to the Fremont Theatre, so I had to convince the guard to go inside and check that everyone was all right. When he came back he said sheepishly, "Mr. Sinatra says to let you in."

"Thanks."

As we entered the theater Jerry said, "I coulda got us in."

"I know."

"Just smack the shit outta him and walk right by," he added.

"I got it, Jerry. That might've been quicker, but this was easier."

In the theater a dress rehearsal was going on and the Sinatra who approached us was decked out in full tux.

"What's goin' on, Eddie?" he asked.

"Have you seen Lily, Mary's sister?"

"No," he said, "I told you —"

"I mean today, either at the hotel or here?"

"No," he said. "Why would she come here?"

"What about Mary?" I asked. "This is important, Frank. Have you heard from her?"

"If I heard from her why wouldn't I tell you?" he demanded. "I'm the one who asked you to find her, remember? What's goin' on with you, Eddie?" He looked at Jerry, as if he had the answers, but got nothing back, not even a shrug.

"Frank, I'm thinking these two girls are trying to pull something."

"Girls? You mean Mary and her sister?" He looked at me as if I was crazy. "What would they be tryin' to pull? Mary's the one in trouble."

"Somebody may be trying to kill her, but the sister is involved, somehow. She showed up here claiming to have just arrived, but she's been here for days. And now she's disappeared, too."

"Look, I've got to rehearse this show," he said, jerking his thumb at the stage. At the moment Sammy Davis was tap dancing while Dino, Joey and Peter Lawford watched him. "We'll be here most of the morning. If you find out anything call me. Otherwise I'll be in my suite until show time."

He looked at Jerry again, but got stonewalled. As he turned and walked back to the stage it was the first time I ever really felt that Jerry was totally on my side, and not conflicted between me, Frank and MoMo.

"Let's go," I said, and Jerry followed me up the aisle and out, giving the guard a good, hard look on the way.

FIFTY-TWO

I felt like I was going in circles. How many
more times could I ask Frank Sinatra if he'd
seen or heard from his girl? He was right, if
he had heard he would have told me. I was
just spinning my wheels because I didn't
know what the hell to do.

"What about the money?" Jerry asked.

"Hmm? What money?" I was leaning on
my arm, looking at the passing scenery
without seeing it.

"The Western Union money," he said.
"The money the sister sent?"

I turned my head and looked at him.

"What?" he asked.

"I don't think there is any money, Jerry," I
said. "At least, not a lot."

"But when we went to the office the guy
told you there was."

"I think Lily sent some money for us to
watch, and chase," I said. "I don't think
Mary ever intended to pick it up."

300

"They were just tryin' ta get you out of the way?"

"Me, or whoever was looking for her. I don't think they knew who it was until I told them."

"When you called her in Chicago?"

And there was that problem again. How could I have spoken to Lily in Chicago if she was in Vegas?

Well, the easiest answers are the best, so it probably wasn't Lily I had spoken to, but someone else. A third girl in on . . . on whatever it was they were in on.

"Three broads?" Jerry said when I told him my thoughts. "That's way out there, Mr. G., what kinda scam could they be pullin'?"

"The best kind, Jerry," I said. "They're scamming somebody for money."

"Better not be Mr. Giancana," he said. "He wouldn't like that."

"Not Giancana," I said, "and not Frank. Somebody else."

"Like who?"

"Like maybe Lily's boyfriend's boss, if she was telling the truth about him."

"You think she stole his money and he sent those boys here to get it back, and kill her . . . and her sister?"

Scenarios were swirling in my head, now.

What if Mary was the innocent sister when it came to the cash? What if she really did come here just to see Frank, but the sister came barging in with the money, and a couple of torpedoes on her ass?

"Ah, what do I look like, a detective?" I asked. "Maybe the guy's wife found out they were playin' slap-and-tickle at work and she sent those hitmen."

"A woman would do that," Jerry said. "Women are meaner than men, ya know?"

I stared at him.

"It's a fact."

"Sometimes you scare me, Jerry."

He sulked for a minute then said, "I know some stuff."

Back at the Sands I checked in for messages with the desk staff of the hotel. I was hoping to hear from Danny as soon as possible. There were none. I decided to make some phone calls and for that I needed a desk.

"I have to go upstairs and borrow somebody's desk," I told Jerry. "You want to hang around down here?"

"And do what?"

"Play the horses?"

"Don't feel like it."

"Watch some blackjack?"

His eyes brightened.

302

"I could go stare at that guy some more for ya."

"There's an idea," I said. "Do that for a while, then go into the lounge and wait for me. Buddy Hackett's gonna be in there tonight."

"He's funny," Jerry said. "I ain't never seen him in person, though."

"He's even funnier," I said. "So I'll meet you in the lounge."

"When?"

"Give me an hour."

"Who ya gonna call?"

"I'm going to check on this airline stub," I said. "And a few other things."

"What floor are ya gonna be on? Just in case."

I told him the offices of the hotel and casino were on the second floor. He headed into the casino and I went to the elevator.

Marcia Clarkson was pretty despite brown hair that was always kind of frizzy. She wore thick glasses but they only served to magnify the beautiful blue of her eyes. In her mid-thirties, one might have called her mousy, but I knew her better than most. We'd gone out a few times and now we were friends.

"Hey, beautiful," I said, sticking my head in her office.

"What do you want?" she demanded.

303

"A desk and a phone for about an hour," I said, easing into the room. "That's all."

"You gonna call that rat?"

I had fixed her up with Danny Bardini six months ago and that hadn't gone well.

"No," I said, "I'm not going to call Danny. I swear."

"Use that one in the corner," she said, pointing with her pen. "It's empty. We're still trying to hire somebody."

"Thanks, Marcia," I said. "You're the best."

"Yeah, yeah, just don't try to fix me up with any more of your friends." Her tone was stern but I saw a hint of a smile on her face.

"Scouts honor," I said. "Never again."

"Were you ever a Scout?" she asked.

"In Brooklyn?" I asked. "That's what you do right after you join a gang."

I walked over to the empty desk, sat down and pulled out the airline ticket stub. She had flown in on Pan Am, and I could make out a phone number for them in faint blue print.

I made the call and after being passed on several times I finally determined that a Lily D'Angeli did fly in on that flight from Chicago on July twentieth. When I asked if someone could describe her to me I was told that no one could. Apparently, that wasn't part of their job.

"What if I was a policeman?" I asked.

"If you were," the woman on the other end said dryly, "you would've said so in the first place."

"Listen —" I started, but she hung up. I stared at the phone for a few seconds, than slammed it down.

"Girl trouble?" Marcia asked.

"You might say that."

"She hung up on you?"

"That was Pan Am," I said. "One of their rude employees. I think I'll make a complaint."

I picked up the phone and dialed Danny's number, even though I'd told Marcia I wasn't going to. It didn't matter because he didn't answer.

I hung up and stared into space.

"Earth to Eddie."

I looked over at Marcia.

"Poor Eddie," she said, leaning her elbows on her desk, "you look like you've got the weight of the world on your shoulders."

Before I could answer, a man walked in, looked at Marcia, winked, then looked over at me.

"They told me you might be up here, pally," Dean Martin said.

305

FIFTY-THREE

"Hey, Dean."

He looked back at Marcia again, who was staring at him with her mouth open.

"Don't I know you?" he asked.

"M-me?"

"I never forget a pretty girl," he told her. "You came to one of my shows? Came backstage?"

"S-s-six months ago," she said. "You and . . . the others. You remember that?"

"You were with his friend," Dino said, pointing first to her and then to me. "The private eye."

"More like private rat," she said, then quickly added, "oh, no offense, Mr. Martin."

"Dean," he said, "call me Dean, and none taken. We don't even call ourselves by that name. That's all in the tabloids." He stared at her some more, then asked, "Marcia, right?"

She looked like she was going to faint. "Y-yes."

"Marcia, can I talk to our friend here in private for a minute?"

"Private? Oh, oh, of course."

She stood up and came around the desk. As she approached Dean and the door he grabbed her hand and kissed it.

"Thanks, doll."

I had the feeling I was going to be forgiven for setting Marcia up with Danny.

After she left, Dean closed the door. There were two other desks in the room besides mine. We were in the offices of the employment department. Apparently, everyone was out except Marcia — who actually ran the whole place.

"Aren't you supposed to be at rehearsal?" I asked. He'd obviously come from there, since he was wearing his tux.

"I rehearsed plenty. I've got it down pat. What the hell is up with Frank?" Dean asked, without rancor. He was obviously curious, and concerned.

"Dean, how much did you know about Frank's problem when you asked me to help him?"

"Everything," he said.

"All of it?" I asked. "The girl, MoMo —"

"Yeah, all of it," he said. He looked

around, then perched a hip on Marcia's desk. "Frank's problem is usually women. Ava — he'll never let that one go — Juliet, and now this new one, Mary."

"Do you know about Lily, too?"

Dean frowned. Apparently not, and he didn't like not knowing.

"Who's Lily?"

"Mary's sister."

"Frank's involved with her, too?"

"I think it's more complicated than that."

I went on to explain it all to Dean, laying everything out. I thought maybe he'd have a fresh perspective.

He listened and when I finished he said, "You need to know some more about this other girl, the sister."

"Yeah," I said. "I'd like to know who this boss is she's been fucking, and then ripping off."

He pointed to the phone on Marcia's desk and asked, "Can I use that?"

"Sure," I said. I doubted Marcia would ever clean it, again.

He picked up the phone, dialed a bunch of numbers and then said, "Fred, it's me. I need a quick check run on . . ." he snapped his fingers at me.

"Lily D'Angeli," I said. "Chicago."

He repeated the name.

"I want to know where she lives, works, who she works for, everything. I'm at the Sands. Call me in my room, or at this number." He read it off to whoever he was talking to and then hung up.

I stared at him. I didn't have the heart to tell him Danny was already working on it. Besides, maybe his guy would get the info first.

"It might take a while. If I get the call in my suite I'll find you." He checked his watch. "I've got time before the show to take a nap."

"Will you be at the premier?" I asked.

"I'll be at the show after," he said, standing up. "I don't want to see the movie."

"Why not?"

"We were a bunch of one-take-Charlies on that shoot," he said. "Let's just say it ain't my best work and leave it at that."

He opened the door.

"Dean?"

"Yeah?"

"Who was on the other end of the phone?"

He studied me for a minute, then said, "Fred Otash." The Hollywood P.I., I thought. "He'll get the goods on this D'Angeli broad, and I'll get it to you. Nobody has to know where it came from, though. *Capice?*"

FIFTY-FOUR

When I came back downstairs I went outside to question the valets, which I should have done in the first place. I used the photo I had of Mary, telling them to imagine her with brown hair.

I'd left Marcia's office with Dean before she returned. He took the elevator up, while I took it down.

"Check in with me later," he said. "Fred's real good at this and I'm sure he'll have something."

"Okay, Dean," I said. "Thanks."

"Anything for Frank," he said, shaking my hand, then added, "or for you, pally."

As his elevator doors closed I tried not to show how pleased the remark made me feel. Foolish, but pleased.

None of the valets remembered Lily getting into a cab, or a car. I went back inside and found Jerry sitting in the lounge, laughing at Buddy Hackett. I stood there for a minute and watched the big guy. I didn't think I'd ever seen him that happy before. I hated to bother him, so I went in search of a house phone instead and called Entratter's office. He'd still be there for a couple of hours. He never left before five.

"Where the hell have you been?" he demanded. "I've been tryin' to find you."

Rather than try to explain what I'd been doing I gave him an answer that would satisfy him.

"I was with Frank, and then Dean."

"Your girl picked up her Western Union money."

I was stunned.

"She couldn't have," I said. "Why would she do that if her sister's here?"

"That ain't for me to figure out, is it, kid?" he asked.

"Did your man follow her?"

"He did, why do you think I been tryin' to find you? Here's the address."

"Wait, wait . . ." I patted myself down, looking for something to write on. I had a pen, but the only slip of paper I had was that airline ticket stub. I smoothed it out and said, "Go."

He read off an address and I wrote it down.

"Do you know where that is?" he asked.

"I do."

"Good, cause I ain't got a clue." I wanted to say, that's because you never leave the Sands, but I shut my mouth.

"Get this done, Eddie," he said. "The opening's tonight."

"Premier."

"What?"

"It's called a premier."

"I don't give a crap what it's called," he said, "I don't want it ruined. Got me?"

"I gotcha, Jack."

I hung up and went to drag Jerry away from Buddy Hackett.

"That was funny," Jerry said, from behind the wheel of my Caddy, "the way Buddy picked on you as soon as you came in."

"Yeah," I said, "it was funny."

I didn't like being the butt of the joke, but I did interrupt Buddy as I entered, taking some of the attention off him, so I guess I deserved it. Jerry thought it was hilarious.

"Where we goin'?" he asked.

"Drive along here a few more blocks, and then turn left."

"We just went past that Western Union office."

"I know," I said. "The girl apparently picked up her money."

"I thought that was just a scam."

"So did I," I said. "I guess we're gonna find out for sure."

He took the turn I told him to and we started looking for the address Jack had given me. At one point Jerry started to chuckle but I didn't bother asking him what he found so damn funny.

"There it is."

This area of Vegas was run-down, to say the least. What we were pulling up in front of was a fleabag hotel.

"She's stayin' here?" Jerry asked.

"That's what I was told."

We got out of the Caddy and entered the lobby of the hotel.

"No vacancy," the kid behind the desk said. "Can't ya read?"

"Believe it or not," I said, "we don't want a room."

"Whataya want?" The acne scars on his face were red, like freckles. And he had a couple of new pimples that were about to burst.

"We're looking for a girl."

"We don't allow none of that here."

"Furthest thing from my mind," I said. I took out the photo of Mary. "Either her, or somebody who looks like her, but with brown hair."

His eyes widened when he saw the photo, and then he quickly hid the fact that he'd recognized Mary Clarke.

"What room?"

"I didn't say —"

"Jerry."

Jerry's hand shot out and he grabbed the guy by the front of his grimy t-shirt. When he pulled, the guy came halfway across the desk until his shirt tore.

"What room?" Jerry asked.

"F-fourteen," the clerk stammered. "Third floor."

"When's the last time you saw her?"

"T-this mornin'. She w-went out."

"She come back?" Jerry asked.

"Not yet."

I touched Jerry on the arm and he let the kid go.

"Be here when we come back down," I told him.

Jerry showed the kid his index finger and said, "Don't make me come lookin' for you."

"I — I'll be here."

"And don't call upstairs," I said, eyeing the switchboard behind the desk.

"I — I won't."

The dump had an elevator, but it didn't work, so we walked. I took the lead. When

315

we got to three I was breathing hard. Jerry was fine. Jesus, I thought, two flights of stairs? I was going to have to get into some kind of shape.

We walked down the hall to fourteen and Jerry pressed his ear to the door.

"Nothin'," he mouthed.

I thought I should have gotten a key from the frightened clerk. Then I decided to try the doorknob and it turned.

"That's not good," Jerry said, taking out his gun. "Me first, Mr. G."

I didn't argue.

I opened the door and Jerry went through the doorway with his gun extended. His bulk blocked my view as he stopped just inside.

"Jerry?"

"Step in carefully, Mr. G.," he said.

I was about to ask why when he stepped aside and I saw the blood.

A lot of it.

FIFTY-FIVE

"We've been in this situation before," Jerry said.

"Too many damn times," I answered.

It was one room, with a bed and some furniture and no place to hide. There was blood on the bed, the floor and the walls, enough to suggest that a helluva fight had gone on and somebody had gotten seriously hurt.

The room was empty.

"Back out," Jerry said, and we did. In the hall he holstered his gun.

"I didn't see any suitcases," I said. "Did you?"

"No."

"The clerk said she went out this morning and hasn't come back."

"Maybe we better talk to him again."

"Yeah," I said, "about a lot of things."

We went down the hall to the stairwell without running into anybody, and the only sounds we heard came from room nine, where a man and a woman and some bed springs were making a hell of a racket . . .

When we got downstairs the clerk was gone.

"I thought we scared him into waitin'," Jerry said.

"I think we scared him into running."

"So now what?"

"We should call the cops."

"You know what'll happen if we do that."

"You can leave, Jerry," I said. "I'll call Hargrove direct and —"

"That man hates you, Mr. G.," Jerry said, cutting me off. "It ain't healthy the way he hates you — for you or for him."

I'd never given serious thought before to the possibility that someone might hate me — and hate me that much. It was unsettling.

"I think one of them anonymous calls would be better," Jerry said.

"You don't think he'll know it's me?"

"Maybe," he said, "but he can't prove it."

No one else had seen us enter or — hopefully — leave. Then again, it would have been more accurate to say that we hadn't seen anyone. Somebody could have cracked a door and spotted us in the hallway. That was a chance we'd have to take. Also, if the clerk reappeared he'd place us at the scene.

"That clerk is still gonna be runnin' tomorrow," Jerry said, as if reading my mind. "We better get outta here and make the call."

We checked the front and made our way to the car without encountering any of the hotel's other residents.

"Jerry," I said, "from the amount of blood in that room, could somebody be dead?"

"It's possible," he said.

"So where's the body?" I asked. "How'd they get it out with nobody seeing them?"

"We got in and out with nobody seeing us."

"Yeah, but we weren't dragging a body."

We drove in silence for a while, then Jerry said, "Wanna stop at a pay phone?"

"Guess that'd be best."

He waited until we were on Flamingo and then pulled over to the curb in front of a Terrible Herbst service station. I didn't get out, because something had just occurred to me.

"What is it?" Jerry asked.

"The blood."

"What about it?"

"There was none in the hall and none on the door," I said.

"None on the window, either."

I looked at him.

"I noticed," he said.

"How'd they get the bloody body out?"

"Wrapped it in somethin'."

"Maybe," I said, "but maybe there was no body."

"Whataya mean?"

"I mean a lot of blood splashed around to make it look like somebody was killed."

"Why?"

"Maybe so we'll stop looking."

"If the cops think somebody's dead they're gonna keep lookin'."

"Maybe," I said, going on with my "maybes," "whoever left the blood isn't worried about the cops. Maybe they're just worried about us."

"Or you," he said. "Ain't nobody worried about me."

"Okay, me," I said. "The blood is to throw me off."

"But the money —"

"Picking up the money at the Western Union office was just a ploy to get me to that hotel, so I'd see the blood. Maybe they figured I'd tell Frank the girl's dead."

"Who's they?"

"That's the question."

"Are we still gonna call the cops?"

"Sure," I said, "why not? Let them deal

with the phony blood trail. It'll keep them off our backs for a while."

"If it's phony."

"Think about it," I said. "You saw the room. If somebody was really dead would there be more blood? Or less?"

"That depends on how they were killed," he said. "If they was stabbed bad they'd bleed like a pig."

"That much?"

"More," he said. "If they was gut-shot they'd bleed to death."

"So, more blood."

"Yeah."

"Could you cut somebody, get a lot of blood and not kill them?"

"Sure."

"I know these two women are up to something," I said. "I feel it now."

"There's another question, though," Jerry said.

"What's that?"

"If nobody's dead," he said, "where'd they get all the blood?"

321

FIFTY-SIX

I called the cops and then got back into the car.

"Where to?" Jerry asked.

"My place," I said. "We've got to get dressed for the premier."

"We're goin'?" he asked. "Both of us?"

"Yeah, we're goin'," I said. "Maybe one or both of these broads will show up there." I looked at him. "Besides, I haven't had time to get myself a date, so you're it, big guy."

"Just better buy me flowers," he muttered, and pressed the accelerator.

When we arrived there was a woman sitting on my front steps. Her head was slumped down between her shoulders, and her face was covered. We couldn't even see if she had brown hair or blonde.

"Old girlfriend?" Jerry asked.

"Unless I miss my guess," I said, "that's one of the sisters we've been looking for."

"Really?" he asked. "We're lookin' all over and we find her on your front porch? Ain't that what they call irony?"

I looked at Jerry and said, "You impress me every day."

He looked proud.

We approached the girl, who looked up quickly, her eyes wild, her hair even wilder. I found myself looking into the face of Mary Clarke.

"Mary?" I said.

"Are you Eddie Gianelli?" She stared at Jerry as she asked me the question.

"That's right."

"My sister, she . . . she told me to come to you for help."

"I've been looking for you for days," I said.

She was still staring at Jerry, as if she expected him to sprout horns.

"This is my friend Jerry," I said. "He wants to help you, too."

Now she looked past us at the street.

"Can we go inside?"

"Of course."

I used my key to open the door and allowed her to go in first. Jerry brought up the rear, pulled the door shut tightly and checked out the window. He turned to look at me and shrugged.

"If I could freshen up somewhere?" she

asked. "I've been . . . running."

"For quite a while, too," I said. "Bath-room's down the hall, on the right."

She had a purse with her. She held it tightly to her chest and went down the hall.

"I'll make some coffee," Jerry said.

"Good idea."

"Think you're gonna get the whole story now?" he asked.

"To tell you the truth, Jerry, I don't think we'll ever get the whole story."

He nodded sagely and went into the kitchen. I wondered if I should position myself outside the bathroom? Was there a chance that she'd beat it out the back door? If she had come to me for help, why would she?

I remained in the living room and soon the bathroom door opened and she came back down the hall. She'd combed her hair, which looked presentable, if a little greasy; fixed her makeup. But her eyes still ap-peared brittle and she'd already chewed some of the fresh lipstick she'd applied.

"Where's . . ."

"Jerry? In the kitchen. He's a homebody. Thought you could use some coffee."

"I could, actually." She touched her hair with one hand and held her purse tightly with the other.

"Mary, have you seen Lily?"

"Yes."

"Do you know where she is now?"

"No."

"Is she alive?"

She hesitated, then said, "I don't know. Can I sit down?"

"On the sofa," I suggested. "You'll be more comfortable there."

"Thank you."

Her white blouse was soiled, but with something black, not red. She sat and her skirt rode up over her knees. I couldn't see any bloodstains on her, and didn't think she'd washed any off in the bathroom.

She pushed her hair back over her ears with one hand, first one side then the other. It was almost shoulder-length. She always managed to keep one hand on her purse. Remembering what her sister was carrying in hers I wondered, how much money was in there? And was it hers or Lily's?

Jerry came back carrying a tray with the coffeepot and three mugs. He played host, poured her a cup, which she took black. He then put the tray on the coffee table and sat off to one side to observe.

She sipped her coffee, regarding me over the rim of her mug.

"Mary . . . what happened? What's been

happening?"

"First . . . why have you been looking for me? I don't know you."

"Frank asked me to see if you were okay."

"You're friends with Frank?"

For want of a better description of my relationship with Sinatra I said, "Yes."

"He's nice."

"Yeah, he is."

I waited, and then looked at Jerry, who just shrugged.

"Mary . . ."

She put the coffee cup down on the table, finally released the purse and covered her face with both hands. I thought she was crying, but when she lowered her hands her face was dry.

"I don't know," she said. "It wasn't my idea. None of it."

"None of what?"

"It was Lily," she said, as if I hadn't spoken. "Lily's big idea . . ."

"For you to be with Frank?"

"What?" She looked at me, as if seeing me for the first time, then over at Jerry. He seemed to fascinate her.

"Frank? No, not Frank. I'm talking about Vito."

I glanced at Jerry, but he was watching her.

"Who's Vito?"

"Lily's boss," Mary said. "The man she worked for . . ."

". . . and was sleeping with?"

"Yes."

She'd told me his name was Roger. Another lie.

"Vito . . . who?"

"Vito Balducci."

This time when I glanced at Jerry he was looking back at me.

"Chicago mob," he said.

"What? Wait . . . the guy Lily ripped off is with the Mafia?"

"Of course," Mary said. "She didn't tell you?"

"All she told me was that she ripped off her boyfriend, who was married, and who couldn't call the cops because it was already stolen money."

"Mob money," Mary said. "And he needs to get it back or he's a dead man."

"Jesus," I said, "you stole from the mob. What the hell were you broads thinking?"

Before she could answer, the front door exploded inward, coming off one hinge. At the time I thought it was from dynamite or something. It turned out later to simply have been from a kick. But at that moment it didn't matter how it had been opened, only that it had and now men were pouring into my house with guns in their hands, and every intention of using them.

Jerry moved right away. He pulled his gun, reached for Mary, closed his big hand around her shoulder and pushed her to the floor. I was on my own while he was being chivalrous, so I hit the deck myself just as the lead started flying.

FIFTY-SEVEN

Jerry had started pulling the trigger right away, his instincts for survival taking over immediately. I froze, just for a minute, wondering if these guys could be cops. But they never identified themselves, never said a word, and they obviously had bad intentions.

I looked at Jerry, who was leaning over Mary, shielding her with his body while he triggered his .45. The three men who had broken in ducked for cover and began firing their own weapons. I was close to one of them, prone on the floor. We were almost face to face so I grabbed a lamp with a heavy metal base and swung it, catching him on the chin before he could shoot. His eyes rolled up into his head and he fell over, releasing his hold on his gun. I grabbed it. It was a revolver, and I knew he'd already fired a couple of shots. I didn't know how many were left but I pointed the gun at the other two men and fired one shot, anyway. Next thing I knew, I was being grabbed from behind and dragged across the floor. Then I was in the kitchen with Jerry and Mary.

"Get her out the back," Jerry said. "I'll hold them off."

I didn't argue.

"You need this?"

He shook his head.

"I got plenty of ammo. Keep it. You might need it. Now go!"

I grabbed his arm and said, "I'll meet you at the Sands."

"I'll be there, Mr. G."

He turned and went back into the living room. That's when I noticed the wound on his arm seeping blood. He'd already been shot once. I was tempted to go back in and help him. But at that moment Mary sagged against me. I wrapped my free arm around her and dragged her to the back door.

I got her out into the yard and stopped. I could still hear gunfire from inside the house. The Caddy was out front, but there was no way I was going to try for it. My best bet was to go through my neighbor's yard and come out on the street behind us. From there we could get over to a main street, catch a cab to the Sands — and call the cops.

I looked at Mary, who was hanging onto me with one hand and to her purse with the other. Goddamn purse, I wanted to snatch it away from her and toss it into the bushes.

Instead I said, "Are you all right?"

"I — I think so. He — he dragged us both out of that room."

"I know."

"Will he be —"

"That, I don't know," I said, "but we better get out of here. If we get caught, or shot, he's gonna be pissed."

"Shouldn't you help him?"

"He's in his element, Mary," I said, "and I'm gonna take you to mine."

We got lucky and flagged down a cab within a few minutes. I thought about telling him to take me to a pay phone, but instead just told him the Sands. When we got there I dragged Mary into the lobby with me to a phone and called the police. I gave them my address, told them I'd heard shots, and hung up without giving a name. I was going to have to come up with a good explanation for Hargrove about why my house got shot up.

"Come on," I said, grabbing Mary's arm. She was on her last legs and almost fell.

My intention was to put her in a room, maybe the same one as her sister, but at the last minute I changed my mind. Guys with guns seemed to be finding me wherever I went. I decided to try something new.

"Where are we going?" she asked as I pulled her along a hallway.

"You'll see."

We finally arrived in the backstage area behind the Copa Room stage. Dean had been replaced that night by another singer so he could attend the premier if he wanted to. Since the guy on stage did not have Dino's voice or stage presence they were using a lot of girls. As I pulled Mary into the women's dressing room it was deserted except for two girls. I knew both of them.

"Hey, Eddie," Mona Rogers said. "Don't you knock?" She was sitting in front of her dressing table, applying the finishing touches to her makeup.

"Hi, honey," Sheila Robinson said. She had her foot up on a chair and was smoothing the stocking on an impossibly long leg.

"I'm sorry, ladies," I said. "But I have a friend here who needs someplace to hide out."

"Boyfriend troubles, hon?" Sheila asked Mary.

"The worst," Mary said, playing along.

"Empty table in the back, Eddie," Mona said. "The other girls'll be in here soon, though."

"I hope we'll be gone by then. Thanks."

I tugged Mary along and deposited her in a chair in front of a mirror with light bulbs around it. The lights were off, but there was enough for Mary to catch sight of herself and gasp.

"We need to talk, Mary," I said. "Right now."

"Are we safe here?" she asked.

I had a quick flash of Jerry pulling me out into the hall and blasting Capistrello — or Favazza, whichever one it was. "Safe enough."

"I really need a shower," she said. "And some clean clothes."

"I can supply the shower later," I said, "and probably a robe."

"Please," she said, "a shower and a robe would be so wonderful. . . ."

"Like I said, later."

"I don't suppose you could include some deodorant?"

Women.

FIFTY-EIGHT

"We don't have much time. What's in your bag, Mary?" I asked.

She looked at me. Then down at the bag, clutched to her chest.

"What?"

"The purse," I said. "Even when we were being shot at you wouldn't let it go. What's in it?"

"It's — it's got my . . . things."

"Things?" I repeated "You mean, like money?"

"A few dollars."

"Not fifty thousand, like your sister?"

"Lily . . ."

"Where is Lily, by the way?"

"I told you, I don't know. We . . . split up."

"Why?"

"We thought it would be safer."

"Whose blood was in that hotel room?"

"Blood?"

"That fleabag hotel you were staying in.

The desk clerk saw you leave, and when we went up, there was blood everywhere."

She put her hands up to her face and said, "Lily?"

"We don't know whose blood," I said. "I thought you might."

She dropped her hands.

"How would I know?"

"Look, Mary," I said, "the truth has to come out some time. Just what were you and your sister trying to pull?"

"I told you, it was all her idea."

"Stealing the money from Balducci?"

"Yes," she said. "She met him at the Ambassador."

"You were the one working there."

"She used to come in with . . . men."

"You met a lot of men there," I said. "Frank, Sam Giancana. Who met Balducci first?"

"I did," she said, "but Sam was showing interest in me, and that scared Vito. Then I introduced him to Lily."

"Wait," I said, "I thought she was his bookkeeper."

"He hired her after a few dates."

"That's not how I used to get my jobs."

"You were a bookkeeper?" She looked surprised.

"A certified CPA, once upon a time, but

335

that's not important now. So Lily went to work for Balducci. Did she know he was mobbed up?"

"He just said he kept the books for them," she said. "She didn't think he was actually a mobster."

"How long did she work for him before you two hatched this plan?"

"About three months, sleeping with him for two . . . and it wasn't my plan. It was hers. I told you that."

"Yeah, you did," I said. "But I've got to warn you, I'm gonna have a lot of trouble believing everything you tell me. Your sister started out lying to me, playing the innocent."

"She does that with men."

"And you don't?"

"I don't lie like her."

"Who do you lie like?"

She firmed her chin and said, "I don't lie a lot, the way she does."

"You don't lead men on?"

She squirmed.

"That's not lying, not really."

"What do you call it?"

"That's the game," she said. "The game men and women play. You don't play games with women?"

"I tend to be brutally honest," I said.

"You must not have a girlfriend."

"Not at the moment, but we're getting off the path again. Tell me what happened at the Golden Nugget, and what it has to do with your sister and Vito Balducci."

"I was only supposed to come to Vegas to see Frank. My sister decided this was the time to hit Balducci for the money he kept in a safe in his office."

"Fifty grand?"

She hesitated, then said, "A hundred."

"He kept a hundred large of mob money in his safe? And she knew the combination?"

She nodded.

"He bragged about it in bed. Lily says men are so stupid."

"Sounds to me like Lily's right."

"Lily's always right."

She said it in a toneless way that did not give away her meaning. I couldn't tell if she really believed it or not.

"Keep going."

She took a deep breath, let it out in a sigh.

"Lily stole the money. She gave me half."

"Generous sister."

"She wasn't giving me half," she said, correcting me. "She gave me half to hold for her. I was supposed to give it back to her here, in Vegas."

"And?"

"And she didn't show up at the Golden Nugget."

"But somebody else did."

"Yes. Two men. They said they were from Mr. Balducci, and they wanted his money. I told them I didn't have it, but they wouldn't believe me."

"Did they look for it?"

"They were going to," she said, "but one of them took off, leaving me with the other guy."

"Why would they do that? Split up?"

She lifted her chin and looked at me.

"I believe he meant to rape me."

"Oh." I've never understood the relationship between rape and pillage. What is the mentality that tells a man to stop what he's doing — especially if he's pillaging — to rape a woman? That mentality is alien to me — and, hopefully, to most men.

"I wasn't going to let him do that."

"So you killed him?"

"I didn't mean to," she said. "I told him I had to go to the bathroom."

"He followed you?"

"Not right away," she said, "but I . . . called out to him and . . . enticed him in."

"And?"

"And I hit him with the top of the toilet tank."

"That's pretty heavy."

"I told you, I was not about to be raped."

"And then you replaced it?"

"Yes."

"That was smart. I don't think the cops have figured out what the murder weapon was, yet."

"It was not murder," she said. "It was self-defense."

"And then you put him in the bathtub?"

She made a face and hugged herself, but said, "Yes. Then I got out of there before the other man came back."

"And somebody helped you get out of the hotel without being seen," I said. "Dave Lewis?"

"Yes, he said that was his name, and that he was the house detective. He said it was his job to help guests." She paused a moment, then said, "I think he expected sex in return for his help."

Yeah, I thought, that would be Dave.

"Did you tell him about the men?"

"I told him two men were after me," she said. "I did not tell him I had killed one of them."

"He must have been surprised when the body was found in the tub."

"Yes," she said, "he was very angry. He had taken me to his apartment to hide me.

339

I was able to fend him off at first, but when he came back after the body was found he was mad and said I owed him."

"And?"

She didn't answer.

"Did you kill him too, Mary? What'd you bash him with?"

"I didn't mean to kill him," she said. "It was . . . some sort of trophy he kept by the bed."

"You gonna tell me it was self-defense?" I asked. "He was still dressed."

"I was . . . undressing for him, and then he told me to undress him. He was a horrible little man, but he got me out of the hotel. I was actually . . . considering having sex with him, but I couldn't do it. When I told him that, he got angry and grabbed me." She rolled up a sleeve so I could see bruises on her upper arm, then covered herself again. Those bruises could have gotten there any number of ways over the past few days, but I didn't say anything.

"So I grabbed the first thing I could find, and I hit him."

"I saw the body, Mary," I told her. Small lie. "He had to have been hit more than once to have that much damage."

"I — I don't know," she said, shaking her head. "I only know that I hit him, and ran."

"Ran where?" Is there another helpful man lying dead somewhere, I wondered?

"I don't know," she said. "I didn't have much money."

"You had fifty thousand dollars!"

She shook her head.

"That was Lily's money. She would have killed me if I used it."

FIFTY-NINE

Was she that afraid of her sister? If so then Lily really had me fooled.

"Okay, so what did you do?"

"I called her," she said. "Collect."

"And?"

"She got mad, said I was ruining everything. She told me to lay low until she got here."

"Did she tell you why she was still at home?"

"She said she had some trouble with Vito, but she had handled it."

I wondered what that meant.

"So I found a cheap hotel — that hotel you were talking about." She shuddered. "The clerk thought I was a hooker. Tried to get me to pay with sex. What is it with men and sex?"

I didn't know if she was really asking me, or if the question was rhetorical. Either way I didn't have time to answer.

"She said she'd send me some money through Western Union that I could use."

"What was wrong with the fifty grand?" I asked. "Was it marked?"

"I don't know. I only know she told me not to use any, even if my life depended on it."

"And you didn't?"

Her head was down most of the time. Now she raised it and looked me in the eyes.

"I'm used to doing what Lily tells me to do, Eddie. After years and years of it."

"So, you are afraid of her?"

"I suppose so," she said. "Or it may just be a reflex. Do you have any brothers or sisters? Older ones?"

"None," I lied. That was a reflex, too — and another story.

"Then you can't know."

I had nothing to say to that.

"I did as she told me, stayed in that hotel and waited."

"And?"

She covered her face with her hands.

"I'm so tired." She dropped her hands and looked at me. "Can we finish tomorrow?"

I wanted to force her to keep going, but I was bone tired myself, and worried about Jerry.

"Okay," I said. "We're missing the movie

tonight, and the show after it, but I'll get to Frank and tell him you're here —"

"Please don't," she snapped.

"Why not?"

"I — Frank's a nice man, and it was very flattering, and exciting, to get attention from him, but . . ."

"But what?"

"Well . . . he's too old for me."

"And MoMo isn't?"

"Mr. Giancana?" she asked, her eyes wide. "I never — there was never anything between Mr. Giancana and me."

I studied her to see if she was telling the truth.

"In fact . . . I've never even been to bed with Frank," she added.

Suddenly, I believed her. I had a picture of Sinatra and Giancana as two middle-aged men telling stories to each other about the sexy blond hat check girl. It wasn't a particularly flattering picture.

"I have to tell him you're all right, Mary."

"But not the rest? Not about Lily and the money?"

I thought a moment, then said, "I'm not sure. I'll have to give it some thought, see where my responsibilities lie."

"It really doesn't concern him, after all," she said. "The stolen money, I mean."

"I guess you're right."

"Thank you."

"But I still have to think about it."

"All right."

"Now listen . . . you can't take off again," I told her. "You have to stay here."

"Where am I going to go?" she asked. "But do you mean here, in this dressing room?"

I nodded. "Until I come and get you."

"But the girls —"

"The girls will watch over you. I've got to find out if Jerry's all right."

"I hope he is."

"I'll be back soon. Try to relax. You should be safe here. Later I'll get you a room and you can get some sleep. Tomorrow we'll have to talk about finding your sister. I'm sure Balducci still wants his money back, and that still puts the two of you in danger."

"Thank you for your help, Eddie."

I decided Mona was my best bet. Sheila was a little too into herself, like a lot of the girls.

"Mona, I've got to leave Mary here for a while."

"Your little girlfriend?"

"She's not —"

"Relax, Eddie, I'm just kiddin'."

"I need you to keep an eye on her."

She turned away from the mirror. Her face was about as perfect as it could be. She was in her early thirties, and in daylight without makeup looked it. On stage, however, she was gorgeous. On stage they were all gorgeous in Vegas.

"Keep an eye on her, as in, make sure she's okay? Or as in, don't let her leave?"

"The second one."

"What's this about, Eddie?"

"Let me just say that Frank Sinatra and Dean Martin will be very appreciative."

"Dino," she said, with a smile. "I love workin' with him. One of them her boyfriend?"

"No. Can you do this for me?"

"Sure, Eddie." She shrugged her bare shoulders. "Why not?"

"I'll be back as soon as I can."

"I'm outta here in a couple of hours," she warned.

"If I can't make it I'll send somebody for her."

"Okay," she said, again. "When I have to go onstage I'll get one of the other girls to help me."

"Thanks, Mona," I said. "I owe you."

"No kisses," she said, covering up. "You'll smudge my face."

"You're the best."

I got out of there.

SIXTY

She had admitted to killing two men. I should have been on the phone to the police as soon as I left her. But if any part of her story was true, and she was one of those women who brought *that* out in men, then her self-defense story might hold up in each case. Certainly the first one.

The other thing on my mind was letting Entratter know what was going on before he left for the Fremont Theatre. A check of my watch told me the movie was due to start in an hour. I had actually wanted to see it, but that was going to have to wait.

The other reason I wanted to call Entratter was because of Jerry. If the cops responded to my house in time to find him there, it would fall to Jack Entratter to get him out of jail — again.

If he was alive.

I found a house phone and called Entratter's suite. He told me he was getting dressed and to come on up.

"What the hell did you and that big Jew bastard do now?" he demanded as he opened the door of his suite to me. "Big Jew bastard" was almost an affectionate term coming from him.

"What do you mean?"

"Well, first of all, look at you."

I was a mess, sure. I hadn't had time to change since leaving my place.

On the other hand, I had never seen Entratter looking so spiffy. He usually refused to wear a tuxedo, but he was in one now — all but the tie, which was hanging loose around his neck.

"We had a little trouble —"

"I heard," he said, cutting me off.

"From who?"

"Jerry," he said. "He called here all worried about you. I hadda tell him I didn't know what was goin' on, since I hadn't heard from you."

"Where is he?" I demanded. "How is he? I thought he caught a bullet —"

"He did," Entratter said. "I sent him to a doctor — a special doctor."

A mob doctor who would treat him without reporting it.

"What about my house?"

348

"Shot to pieces, apparently," he said. "The cops are lookin' for you to ask you about it."

"Hargrove?"

He nodded, fiddling with his tie with his sausagelike fingers.

"He didn't catch the squeal, but when he heard about it he bought in."

"Great."

"You goin' to the premier?"

"That was my original plan."

"What's keepin' ya?"

"I found the girl."

He'd been standing in front of a mirror, still fighting with his tie, and now he turned and stared at me.

"What?"

"Jerry didn't tell you?"

"He didn't tell me nothin' except you and him were in your house, some goons broke in and started shootin'." He dropped his hands to his sides. "I think you better tell me what the fuck is goin' on."

"Well . . ."

"So there's two broads? Sisters?" he asked after hearing me out.

"That's right."

"And we got one of 'em. Frank's girl."

"That's right."

"And the two of them ripped off a mob bookkeeper from Chicago."

"Right."

He shrugged and turned back to the mirror.

"Are you gonna tell —"

"Tell who? And what? Some Chicago family got careless with their dough. It ain't MoMo, so it's no skin off my nose. You gonna find this other one? The sister?"

"Tomorrow, hopefully."

"And alive, hopefully," he added.

"Yeah."

"Okay, well, go get dressed."

"What for?"

"You're comin' ta the show."

"I don't have time —"

"You got time to make the show after, maybe even some of the movie. Frank and Dean want you there, and I want you there."

"Jack," I said, "I've got to talk to Jerry, find Lily —"

"Tomorrow," he said. "All tomorrow. Tonight we make nice to Frank, Dean and the guys."

This was crazy. An hour ago I was getting shot at, and now I was supposed to go to the movies?

"You still got the suite," he said. "Take a shower, get dressed and meet me at the theater."

"Jack —"

"Don't screw with me, Eddie," he said. "I ain't in the mood." He dropped his hands again, turned to me and shouted, "And can you tie this fuckin' tie?"

SIXTY-ONE

My tux was in my locker. I took it to the suite with me, showered and started to dress. I was doing my cuffs when the phone rang.

"Mr. G.? You okay?"

"Jerry? Hey, big man, it's great to hear your voice. You saved my life again tonight."

"Just doin' my job."

"Yeah, right. How are you?"

"Not bad. Bullet grazed me, but it's just a scratch. I've had worse. How's the girl?"

"She's okay."

"Get anythin' outta her?"

"Enough." I gave him a rundown. "I'll get the rest tomorrow."

"What about the rest of tonight?"

"Tonight," I said, "I'm going to the movies."

"Can I still come?"

Why not, I thought? I asked him his tux size — he didn't know until I said suit size

— and told him I'd have one sent up.

When Jerry appeared in the lobby I was shocked. The way his suit fit I was expecting the worst — someone who looked even more uncomfortable in a tux than Jack Entratter.

Jerry looked great.

"What?" he asked.

I told him.

"Really? I feel funny."

"Have you ever worn a tuxedo before?"

"No."

I stepped back and looked him up and down.

"You look good, Jerry."

"So do you, Mr. G."

Then I realized what was bothering me. "Who tied your tie?"

"The maid."

I'd made one call and the hotel had sent him the works — shirt, tie, shoes, tux complete with cummerbund — and somebody to tie his tie.

"Shoes okay?"

"Fine," he said.

"How's your arm?"

"Okay. Don't worry about it, Mr. G. Come on, let's go to the movies."

I couldn't believe it but the big guy was

embarrassed.

"Yeah, let's go."

"The Caddy?"

"Let's take a cab," I suggested. "A man in a tux shouldn't drive."

One of the valets outside got us a cab and I told the driver to take us to the Fremont Theatre. I had decided to call Danny from there and have him go and get the girl. At that moment two doors opened and two men got into the cab with us. I didn't protest because they were holding guns. One got in the back next to me, the other in the front.

The one in the front pointed his gun at Jerry.

"Out."

"No."

"I'll kill you right here, Mac."

"I ain't gettin' out."

"Somebody wants to see you," the second man said. He was holding his gun on me. "But they don't want to see him."

"If he don't get out he's dead," the first man said.

"Jerry, get out of the car."

"Mr. G. —"

"Just do it!" I said.

"These guys might kill you."

"They might kill me," I agreed, "but

354

they'll definitely kill you if you don't get out."

"But —"

"Do it," I ordered.

I could see Jerry's mind racing. He was figuring the angles, wondering if he could take both of these guys out without getting me killed. He was thinking about his own safety second.

I put my hand on his arm and said, "Get out, Jerry."

Looking like he wanted to cry he opened the door and stepped out slowly. I had to reach out and close it myself.

The cab driver, who'd been quiet up to this point, asked, "What's goin' on?" He was starting to become alarmed.

The man in the front said, "We're playin' a joke on our friend, here."

"We still goin' to the Fremont Theatre?"

"No," the man said, "but we are goin' downtown. Just drive. I'll tell you where to stop."

"Yes sir."

I looked at the guy in the back seat with me and slid over to put some space between us. The gunman sitting in front had what looked like a boil on the back of his neck. The one sitting with me had the greasiest black hair I'd ever seen.

"Are you takin' me to see Giancana?" I asked.

"Just sit back and shut up," Greasy Hair said. "You'll find out when we get there."

We weren't driving out to the desert, where many bodies have been lost and found, so they apparently really were taking me to talk to someone. I saw no harm in sitting back and doing as I was told.

SIXTY-TWO

Fremont Street was crowded. If there had ever been a movie premier there before, I didn't know about it. There had certainly never been one with Frank, Dean and the rest of the guys in it. It was a big night, especially since they were going to perform afterwards.

"We're going to miss the movie," I said.

"Funny guy," Boil said.

"Stop tryin' to be funny," Greasy Hair said.

"It's a mob scene down here," the cabbie complained.

"We're goin' ta the other end of Fremont," Boil said. "Just keep goin'."

While the El Rancho was the first property to open on the Strip in 1941, the El Cortez opened at the same time downtown. It stood at Sixth and Fremont, about four or five blocks from the Fremont Theatre. Boil told the cabbie to pull around behind the

El Cortez. I wondered how much longer the cab driver had to live? Of course, that depended on whether or not they intended to kill me. If that was the case they couldn't afford to let him go. If I showed up dead tomorrow — or next week, or next month — he'd talk to the cops.

If they let the cabbie go, there was a good chance I'd survive the night.

As we pulled up behind the El Cortez, the headlights briefly illuminated a man standing there. Most of the action was at the other end of the street, at the Fremont Theatre, so it was pretty deserted where we were. Anyone entering the building would be doing so from the front.

The cab pulled to a stop and Greasy said, "Get out."

I opened the door on my side as he opened his. Boil remained in the front. This did not make me or the cabbie very happy. We were both hoping he'd be sent on his way.

We walked to the man, who was now shrouded in the shadows. As we got closer he stepped forward, into the light cast by a nearby lamppost.

"Did you frisk him?" he asked.

"Yeah, we did," Greasy said, which was a lie. He forgot to frisk me and was afraid to admit it. That meant that these were not top boys.

"You the one they call Eddie G?" the man asked.

"That's me."

"My name's Balducci," he said. "They tell me you got this town wired."

"I know some people."

"Yeah, I know you do," Balducci said. "You're supposed to be down the street at that premier, ain'tcha?"

"That's right."

"Well," Balducci said, "there's a chance you won't make it."

"Oh yeah? Why's that?"

He touched his nose. It was a John Barrymore nose. He had the kind of looks most broads went for. That must have been why Lily was able to take him. He was probably shocked that she'd been able to resist his looks and, instead, ripped him off.

"Look where you are, sport."

He may have been handsome, but he wasn't intimidating, and after what I had already dealt with that week, neither were his two boys, Greasy and Boil. Besides, they'd not only forgotten to search me, they never looked behind us to see if Jerry was following.

"I know where I am . . . sport," I said.

"What's on your mind?"

"You've been getting in my way."

"And now you want me out?"

"No," Balducci said. "You're gonna help me."

"Help you what?"

"Get my money back."

"*Your* money?"

He looked me up and down, then looked past me at Greasy.

"Let the cabbie go," he said.

"Yes, sir."

"And give him a real good tip."

Greasy turned, waved at Boil, then rubbed his thumb, forefinger and middle finger together in that universal gesture.

"Mr. Gianelli," Balducci said, "will you join me inside for a drink before you go to the premier?"

"Why not?" I asked. "I'm a little dry after my cab ride."

"Wait out here," Balducci said to his men as the cabbie peeled rubber. "Both of you."

"Yeah," I said, tossing a look over my shoulder as I followed Balducci inside. "Both of you."

SIXTY-THREE

"Where did you get those jerks?" I asked, as he led me to a booth in the coffee shop.

"They got you here, didn't they?"

We had passed a cashier's cage along the way and Balducci had flinched when the man behind the bars called out to me by name. I waved back.

"Guess you know lots of people," he said. I wondered why he was impressed that I was known to a cashier?

"What's to stop me from just walking out the front door?"

He stopped, turned and looked at me.

"I checked you out, Eddie," he said. "You're not a hard guy."

"Neither are you," I said. "You're a bookkeeper."

"A bookkeeper who's got two guys with guns covering the front and the back."

I looked around. The El Cortez was suffering from what was going on down the street at the Fremont Theatre. When the movie started, though, all the people without tickets who were just trying to get a look at Frank and Dean and — if they were in their right minds — Angie Dickinson — would return to the casinos and the tables, and things would liven up. I needed more people in the building if I was going to get out.

"Okay," I said, sliding into a red leather booth, "talk to me."

Balducci slid in across from me. A tired-looking waitress appeared and we both ordered coffee.

"That's all?" she asked.

"I'll take a piece of pie. Apple," I said.

"Nothing for me," Balducci said.

"What a dump," he said, as she left.

The El Cortez might have been the oldest casino in Vegas and, as such, might have been showing some wear, but I didn't agree it was a dump.

"Look," I said, "I've got a movie and a show to go to."

"Where's Mary Clarke?"

"What makes you think I know?"

"I told you, I checked you out."

I stared at him, then leaned back. "Somebody gave you my name."

"You're right. Lily did. And she told me

362

you had Mary stashed away — with my money."

I frowned. That didn't make sense to me. Why would Lily give up me and her sister . . . unless she was trying to hang us out to dry.

"Wait a minute," I said. "Lily stole the money from you, and now she's convinced you that Mary and I have it?"

"Well, she doesn't have it," he argued. "Somebody has to."

"Why me?"

"Why not you?" he demanded. "Are you immune to money and a beautiful girl?"

"Well, we know you're not."

"Look," he said, "why don't I just blast you out of your shoes right now. I know where you live, I know where you work. I'll find it!"

"First," I said, "you tellin' me I'm not a hard guy may be right, but it's like the pot callin' the kettle black."

"What's that supposed to mean?"

"You're not carryin' a gun, Vito," I said, "And another thing . . . your boys forgot to frisk me, and didn't want to admit it."

"You're lyin'."

"Try me."

He studied my face.

"You're trying to tell me you're heeled?"

" 'Heeled.' " I repeated. "The word doesn't even sound right coming out of your mouth."

He stared at me, trying to find some giveaway — a "tell" — on my face. His face was turning red, either from embarrassment, or barely contained rage.

"Look, neither of us has to be hard guys to get this done," he said. "I have to get that money back where it belongs by the middle of the month or I'm dead." He leaned forward. "Yeah, I ain't a hard guy, but I've still got two guys who'll kill you if I tell them to."

"You haven't even got that."

"What?"

"My guy followed us here," I said. "He's the real deal, Balducci. He's probably already taken care of your guys and if I say the word he'll break your legs off at the knees and shove' em up your ass."

"Y— you're bluffing."

"Hey," I said, "this is my town, not yours. Go ahead and try me."

The waitress came with the coffee and my pie. I said thanks and she shuffled back to the counter. Meanwhile, Balducci was still trying to figure me out.

"Goddamn women," he hissed, softly.

"I understand your pain," I told him.

"Women can be . . ."

"Bitches," he said, with a lot of feeling, "goddamned bitches!"

"Yeah, they can be," I agreed. I cut into my pie and tasted it. Not as good as the Sands, but okay.

I hoped I was reading him right and he was reading me wrong. He may have been a Mafia bookkeeper, but he was still just a bookkeeper — maybe even a CPA. But I knew CPAs because I was once one, and we — they — did not carry guns. But this one had gotten somebody to carry them for him. I didn't know what he had promised those men, but even though I was bluffing my ass off, I hoped I was wrong. Maybe Jerry had followed us, and maybe he had already taken care of those two goons.

"Look," he said, "I'll pay you a finder's fee."

Finally, I saw a way out.

"How much of a finder's fee?"

"Ten percent."

"Ten percent of . . . what?" If I'd said, "A hundred grand," then he would have known that I already knew.

"A hundred grand."

I whistled, as if it was the first time I'd heard the amount.

"So that's ten thousand for me?"

"Right."

"And you put the ninety back and nobody's the wiser — and what about my ten?"

"I'll put that in, myself."

I wondered where he'd get *that* ten thousand.

I gave it as much thought as it deserved, then shook my head.

"Sorry," I said, "can't do it, Vito. I wouldn't be able to live with myself."

"Then you ain't gonna live at all." He waved his hand. I turned, hoping he was going to be disappointed, hoping that his boys had run into Jerry outside, but instead I was the one who was disappointed. Greasy and Boil came walking over, their hands inside their jackets on their guns.

"Take him out into the desert and dump 'im." He looked at me. "You coulda been rich, Eddie, but now you're just dead."

"This doesn't make you a mob guy, Vito," I said. "You're still just a bookkeeper."

"Get him out."

The two hoods flanked me. My legs were weak and I didn't know if I was going to make it to my feet. Maybe if they had to drag me out we'd attract some attention. Or maybe I'd just lose my dignity before I lost my life.

I was trying to decide what to do when I

366

saw something that surprised me, especially in the El Cortez, away from the strip.

Because when Sam Giancana was in Vegas, he usually stuck to the strip.

Sixty-Four

I got it. It popped into place. The reason MoMo would even be in Vegas when Entratter wasn't expecting him.

"Holy crap," I said to Balducci, "you stupid sonofabitch, you took MoMo's money?"

He turned in his chair, saw Giancana and four of his men approaching, and then turned back.

"You can't say nothin'," he pleaded with me. "He'll kill me!"

I didn't have time to say anything. Giancana and his men reached us. Greasy and Boil didn't know what to do, but they did drop their hands from their guns. Smart move.

As usual MoMo was wearing dark glasses, even at night. All five of them were wearing dark suits, white shirts and thin ties. They weren't downtown for the premier. They were downtown for this.

"Vito," MoMo said. "How ya doin'?"

"Mr. Giancana," Balducci said, starting to get up, "What are you doin' here?"

"Sit, Vito." Giancana put his hand on Balducci's shoulder. He didn't put any pressure, just laid it there, and the bookkeeper fell back into his chair.

I realized as Giancana's men flanked Balducci that one was Bats. The other three were new to me. Mikey's broken fingers were probably still keeping him out of action.

"Mr. Gianelli," MoMo said to me, "nice to see you again, pal."

"MoMo," I said.

"You boys mind if I join ya?"

"I don't mind," I said. "Do you mind, Vito?"

Balducci looked at me like I was crazy.

"Uh, no, no, I don't mind. Have a seat, Sa— uh, Mr. Giancana."

"Thanks." He turned and spoke to three of his men. "Boys, take these other fellas outside, will ya? Make sure they don't hurt themselves?"

"Sure thing, Mr. Giancana," one of them said.

"Mr. Balducci —" Greasy said, but Vito had his own problems and looked away.

Slickly, MoMo's men disarmed the other

two and walked them outside.

Giancana sat, Bats remained standing. I looked at him and he nodded to me. For some reason, I found that encouraging. Suddenly, my legs did not feel as weak, the situation did not seem as hopeless. Now I just had to hope that Giancana didn't think of a reason to have me taken out into the desert.

"Vito," Giancana said in response to Balducci's question, "I think the question is, what are you doin' in Vegas?"

"Me? I was just, uh, takin' some time off, Mr. Giancana."

"Chicago don't know where you are," MoMo said. "They were gettin' worried."

"Ah, well, they got nothin' to worry about, Mr. Giancana —"

"Well, they seem to think they do," Giancana said. "Seems some money's come up missin'. They seem ta think you can help 'em find it."

"Money?"

"A hundred thousand," Giancana said. He looked at me. "That's a lot of money, even in this town, ain't it, Eddie?"

"It sure is, Mr. Giancana." I remembered what Jerry had told me about respect.

Giancana looked at Balducci.

"Think you can help find the money, Vito?"

"I know I can, Mr. Giancana," he said. "It was that bitch I hired to work for me. She took it."

"How could she get her hands on that much of our money, Vito?" Giancana asked, confirming my theory. Balducci had not only been stupid enough to steal from the Mafia, but from Sam Giancana — and then Lily and Mary had stolen it from him.

"She, uh, she . . ."

Giancana waved his hand in front of Balducci to stop him.

"We can talk about it someplace else, Vito." He looked at me again. "Don't you got a show to go to, Eddie?"

"Yes, sir."

Bats put his hand on Vito Balducci's shoulders.

I went out the front and found Jerry waiting for me.

"You called Giancana."

He nodded.

"I grabbed a cab as soon as you pulled away and followed you all here. Then I called him."

"Why?"

He came as close to pouting as he could

without pushing out his lower lip.

"I was mad at you."

"Mad at me? Why?"

"You made me get outta the car," he said. "I coulda took them two bums. They was nothin'."

"I embarrassed you in front of them?"

He didn't answer.

"I saved your life," I said, "or, at least, I was trying to."

"It ain't your job ta save my life, it's my job ta save yours."

"So now you're saying you're mad at me because I took your job?"

He didn't answer.

"Well, now that MoMo's got Balducci," I said, "we still don't know where Lily is."

"We know where Mary is," he pointed out. "Wasn't that the job Mr. S. wanted you to do?"

"The job got muddled."

"So whatta we do now?"

"You still mad?"

"No."

"Good," I said, "then we might as well go to the movies."

SIXTY-FIVE

We only got to see half the movie, but the whole show afterward. We saw the actual heist — Frank as "Danny Ocean" and his crew taking down a bunch of casinos at one time — and then the aftermath, as everything went wrong. The ending was very clever and proved that, as usual, crime didn't pay.

Unless you were two beautiful sisters.

The stage show went as it usually did, the guys having a great time and the audience loving it. When Jack Entratter saw that I had brought Jerry with me he didn't look happy, but he didn't say anything about it. He just hung with the showbiz types like Tony Bennett and Vic Damone. George Raft was there, too, and gave me a little head bow when he saw me.

There was a party afterward and I took Jerry with me to that, too. He stared at all the stars, especially the women, like Juliet

Prowse, Ruta Lee, and Shirley Maclaine. Producers were present, directors, even some studio heads. Henry Silva, Nick (Richard) Conte and Jerry Lester were off to one side, laughing and holding drinks. Juliet was hanging on Frank's arm, while Frank kept looking over at me. He obviously wanted to get me aside to ask questions.

Sammy Davis and Peter Lawford were standing together, chatting with a couple of honeys who looked like showgirls. I was looking around for Dean Martin when he quietly sidled up to me.

"Hey, pally, how's it goin'?" he asked.

"Dean, just the man I was looking for. Have you met my friend Jerry?"

"Hey, Jerry." Dean shook the big man's hand. Jerry looked starstruck. They had spoken on the phone but never met.

"Frank wants to talk to you," Dean said, "but he can't shake Juliet. She's hangin' tight onto his arm."

"I noticed."

"Any progress?"

"A lot," I said. "We found —"

"Good," Dean said, "but tell Frank, not me. I'll see if I can spring him from his lady."

"Okay."

I looked at Jerry, who was still staring after Dean as he went up to Frank.

"Haven't you met Dean before?"

"No."

"But I thought, working for Frank —"

"I don't know a lot of show-business types, like you do, Mr. G. I've just done some stuff for Mr. S."

I saw Dean lean in and say something to Frank. Then some bodies got in the way and I lost them. Suddenly, a path cleared, but instead of seeing Frank and Dean I saw Detective Hargrove and his partner coming towards me and Jerry with two uniforms. Entratter saw them, too, and came rushing over to intercept them.

"What now, Hargrove?"

"I'm taking Gianelli and his friend downtown, Mr. Entratter."

"Why?"

"Because I'm sick of having bodies turn up."

"Bodies? What body has turned up now?" Jack asked.

"A girl this time."

"Blonde?" I asked, wondering if Mary had left her room at the Sands.

"No, brunette," Hargrove said. "Not the girl you're looking for, but I still think you can help us."

"Why me and Jerry?"

"Because this girl is the other one's sister."

I almost blurted Lily's name, but instead said, "And she's dead?"

"Murdered," Hargrove said, "and you're gonna help me find out who killed her."

"Detective, this is a party —" Jack started.

"For these two," Hargrove said, cutting him off, "the party is over."

Sixty-Six

They took us to see the body first and it was Lily. Somebody had shot her twice. After they showed her to us they took us downtown and put us in separate interview rooms.

I sat in mine alone for about twenty minutes and then Hargrove and Gorman came in. All four walls were blank. No mirrors, no windows, just bile green walls.

Hargrove sat across from me. Gorman leaned against the wall, as usual.

"That girl is dead because of you," Hargrove said.

"How do you figure that?"

"You could have told me about her, and her sister."

"How did you identify her as Mary Clarke's sister?" I asked.

"Her wallet. There was a picture of the two of them. They could just be friends, but the resemblance points more to them being related." He shrugged. "Sisters."

I could have congratulated him, but that just would have made him mad. I didn't want to antagonize him. I wanted this all to be over so I could go back to my Pit.

"What do you know about the murder of Lily D'Angeli?" he demanded.

"Nothing," I said, truthfully. What did I know? Only that she was dead. I knew who had killed the two men — Dave Lewis and one of the goons who had been sent to find her. And Jerry had killed the other bozo. I didn't have any knowledge of who had killed Lily.

Now the question was, did I offer what I knew about the dead men to Hargrove? Did I give Mary Clarke up? That depended on whether I believed her self-defense stories.

"What if I told you big Jerry gave you up?" he asked.

"You know I wouldn't believe that."

"He's pretty loyal, that big sonofabitch." There was almost admiration in his tone.

"Besides that, there's nothing to give up."

"Look," he said, "that girl is still on the run and her sister is dead. Whoever killed Lily has to still be after Mary."

That might've been true, if I hadn't seen MoMo Giancana take Vito Balducci away. It had to be Balducci's men who killed Lily.

Maybe they'd found the money — the share she was carrying — and hadn't told their boss. I wondered what had happened to the two of them? Had Giancana taken care of them, too?

I was waiting for Hargrove's next question when the door opened and a young uniformed cop stuck his head in.

"Detective? Somebody out here wants to see you."

"Well, who is it?"

"I think you better come out here and see."

Hargrove sighed, stood up and went out the door. Gorman stayed where he was.

"How long till retirement?" I asked.

"A month," he said, "give or take."

That explained a lot.

We waited in silence until Hargrove returned, with another man in tow.

"Hey, Eddie," Frank Sinatra said.

"Frank." I was surprised. "What are you doin' here?"

"Came to keep you out of trouble."

"Mr. Sinatra informs me that you were looking for Mary Clarke for him," Hargrove said. "Is that true?"

I looked at Frank, who nodded.

"Yes."

"And you never knew her before."

"No."

"And everything you told me about going to her hotel room is true?"

"Yes."

"And have you seen her since?"

I looked at Frank and got another nod.

"Yes."

"Where?"

"At the Sands Hotel."

"When?"

"Well . . . today."

"She's at the Sands now?" Hargrove asked.

"That's right."

"She's safe?" Frank asked. "Unhurt?"

"Yeah, Frank, she's fine." She killed two men and helped her sister steal a hundred grand of mob money, I thought, but she's fine.

Hargrove looked at Frank.

"You got any objection to us going to the Sands and questioning her?"

"Would it matter if I did?" Frank asked.

"No."

"But you'll stick to your word. This won't get into the papers."

"I said I wouldn't leak it to the papers," Hargrove reminded him. "I can't vouch for everyone in this building. Somebody had to recognize you."

"I understand."

"Let's go, Eddie," Hargrove said.

"Where?" I wondered if he was gonna put me in a cell for some reason.

"We're going to the Sands. You're going to show me this girl."

"I'm comin' along," Frank said.

"And so is Jerry," I added.

"Yeah, fine," Hargrove said. "We'll all go. We'll have a fuckin' party."

Jerry and I drove in the Caddy, but Hargrove insisted Frank go with him and his partner in their unmarked car. Maybe he wanted to question Frank more along the way.

"Mr. S. came to the rescue, huh?" Jerry asked as he drove.

"Looks like it."

"You gonna tell him what his girl and her sister were doin'?"

"I haven't decided yet."

"He thinks she's such a sweet broad, huh?"

"She had him fooled, all right."

Jerry hesitated, then said, "It ain't gonna make him happy to know that she conned him."

I had already thought of that.

When we got to the hotel we parked out

front and all stormed through the lobby together, trying to keep up with Hargrove. Finally, he realized he didn't know where he was going, and he stopped to wait for me.

"Where the hell is she?"

At that moment Danny Bardini came walking across the lobby towards us. I'd managed to call him from the theater after all, but he didn't look like he had good news.

"What's he doing here?" Hargrove demanded.

"I asked him to watch the girl for me."

"Where is she?" he demanded again.

"I stashed her in one of the backstage dressing rooms and had one of the girls watching her."

Danny reached us and gave me a helpless look.

"Tell it," I said.

"She was gone when I got here."

"She was here," I said to Hargrove. "I swear."

"Mona said she slipped out when she went on stage," Danny added.

"She was supposed to watch her, or have somebody watch her."

Danny shrugged. "Whoever she gave that job to fucked it up."

382

"Did she have a suitcase?" Hargrove asked.

"No."

"A bag of any kind?"

"Just her purse."

"And what was in the purse?"

"The usual stuff, I guess," I said, "although she did hold onto it pretty tight."

Hargrove looked at Gorman, who just shrugged, then looked at Frank, who gave him nothing.

"You let her get away," Hargrove said to me.

"I didn't know I was supposed to hold her," I said. "Is she a suspect, or a victim?"

"That's a damn good question," Hargrove said, "and one I'm going to ask her when I find her." He pointed his finger at me. "You hear from her again you call me. Got it?"

"Oh, I got it."

He turned to leave and ran smack into Jerry, who didn't budge. Hargrove angrily went around him and left, followed by Gorman. That left me in the lobby with Frank, Jerry and Danny, and people around us, staring.

"Where is she, Eddie?" Frank asked.

"I swear, Frank," I said, "she was here."

"Why didn't you let me know?"

Well, for one, I thought, she didn't want me to.

"I didn't have time," I said. "Look, Frank, the girl is in trouble, and I don't think she wants to get you involved."

"What kind of trouble?"

"The kind you don't want any part of, Mr. S.," Jerry said.

Frank looked at both of us, back and forth, a couple of times, then folded his arms.

"I've got Juliet Prowse waitin' for me in my room, fellas, but I think somebody better tell me what's been goin' on."

So I told him. . . .

EPILOGUE

May 20, 1998
They lowered Frank Sinatra into the ground.

Tears rolled down my face the way they had when I'd stood at Dean Martin's gravesite three years earlier. Dean had died on Christmas Day, 1995. Sammy died of cancer in 1990. Peter had drunk himself to death by 1984.

And now Frank.

I looked over at Joey Bishop, who looked haggard and shrunken. He was eighty years old, his usually neat and close-cut black hair now a tangled mess of steel wool gray, blowing slightly in the breeze.

With family members standing around me, sniffling and mourning, I thought back . . .

Frank was apparently satisfied that I had seen Mary Clarke and she was all right.

However, hearing that she had been a party to her sister's stealing mob money he relieved me of any further obligation to find her.

"You did what I asked you to do, Eddie," he'd said. "Now forget it." And he went to his suite, where Juliet Prowse was waiting for him. . . .

Forget it? Two sisters rip off a mob book-keeper, who thinks he's a wise guy and hires cheap talent to hunt them down. They all end up dead. The cheap talent, Capistrano and Favazza; Vito Balducci, the bookkeeper, who nobody ever saw again after I left him with MoMo Giancana that night in the El Cortez coffee shop; and both Lily and her sister, Mary Clarke. And there was an un-named accomplice, a woman who had pretended to be Lily D'Angelo speaking to me on the phone from Chicago. It was probably some innocent friend Lily had stuck by the phone, who didn't know what she was getting involved in. Maybe she never found out.

I say two dead women because not only was Lily dead, but Mary Clarke's body was found several months later in a shallow desert grave. No one knew what became of the money she and Lily had stolen from

Vito, but since all three were dead, the assumption was that the money had gone back where it belonged.

And so the dead were forgotten.

Over the years Frank Sinatra never mentioned Mary Clarke to me again. He also never married Juliet Prowse. He did marry Mia Farrow but that didn't last, and finally married Barbara, who was now his widow. However, people who knew him well — better than I did — still insisted that Ava Gardner was the love of his life — and vice versa. But Ava was gone, too.

As the small crowd began to disperse and move away from the grave I drifted along with them. Joey had an assistant who walked along with him, holding him by the elbow. The halcyon days were gone, for the boys, for him, and for me, too.

I was flattered that I had been included with Joey and the family as the only ones to accompany the coffin from Los Angeles to the Cathedral City grave site. The family didn't pay me much mind, except for a nod and a smile from Barbara at the service. The others probably didn't know me. I was only there because Frank had invited me — but that's another story.

I walked to my rental car. My suitcase was in the trunk. One night in a hotel was enough. I had a plane back to Vegas in two hours. Where else would I live, even though the casinos had no use for me now? I had been an honest dealer for years, and then a straight pit boss for many more years. When the Sands was torn down, so was I. I was done working Vegas. Now I just lived there, sustained by my savings, and my memories.

Memories . . . driving to the airport I had nothing to do but sift through my Rat Pack memories, and I remembered Barney Crane. He was the dealer I'd had my buddy Jerry Epstein stare at back in 1960. I'd hoped the attention would stop Barney doing what he was doing. I'd noticed that he was working with a partner, cheating the Sands out of chips at a nonlethal pace. Nonlethal because the Sands wouldn't go broke from what Barney and his cohort were stealing, but Barney would be pocketing some walking-around money.

As I've said before, I hated when players tried to cheat at one of my tables. Arms and legs had been broken in the effort to dissuade them from coming back. But what I hated even more was a dealer, or pit boss, who cheated. And it was a lot easier for a dealer to cheat when he had a pit boss working with him.

After the whole Mary Clarke debacle I'd

gone back to work and the first thing I did was turn Barney and his dealer buddy in to Jack Entratter. Jack told me he'd take care of it.

"You want me to sit in?" I'd asked. Remember, Jack liked his people to follow through on these things.

"Not this time, Eddie," he'd said. "Why don't you just stay clean on this one?"

I never saw Barney Crane or that dealer again. Two more victims of that summer of *Ocean's 11.*

AUTHOR'S NOTE

These Rat Pack books grew out of my respect for Dean Martin, Frank Sinatra, and Sammy Davis, Jr. as entertainers — not necessarily in that order. As always, my posthumous thanks goes out to these three men for years of enjoyment through their films, their albums, and their appearances on stage.

The books also stem from my love for the history, the pulse, the excitement that is Las Vegas. There's no other place in the world like it. This was as true in 1960 as it is true now.

My thanks also to Kathy War, photo archivist, UNLV Libraries, Special Collections Department, for talking with me and providing me with archive photos of the Sands Casino and the boys.

BIBLIOGRAPHY

Rat Pack Confidential by Shawn Levy, Doubleday, 1998; *The Rat Pack* by Lawrence J. Quirk and William Schoell, Harper, 1998; *Dino* by Nick Tosches, Dell Publishing, 1992; *His Way: The Unauthorized Biography of Frank Sinatra* by Kitty Kelley, Bantam Books, 1986; *Gonna Do Great Things: The Life of Sammy Davis, Jr.* by Gary Fishgall, Scribner's, 2003; *The Peter Lawford Story: Life With The Kennedys, Monroe and The Rat Pack* by Patricia Seaton Lawford, Carroll & Graf Publishers, 1988; *Mouse in The Rat Pack: The Joey Bishop Story* by Michael Seth Starr, Taylor Trade Publishing, 2002; *The Frank Sinatra Film Guide* by Daniel O'Brien, BT Batsford, 1998; *The Last Good Time: Skinny D'Amato, The Notorious 500 Club & The Rise and Fall of Atlantic City* by Jonathan Van Meter, Crown Publishers, 2003; *Casino: Love and*

Honor in Las Vegas by Nicholas Pileggi, Simon & Schuster, 1995; *Las Vegas is My Beat* by Ralph Pearl, Bantam Books, 1973, 1974; *Murder in Sin City: The Death of a Las Vegas Casino Boss* by Jeff German, Avon Books, 2001; *Ava Gardner: Love Is Nothing* by Lee Server, St. Martin's Press, 2006.

ABOUT THE AUTHOR

Robert J. Randisi is the founder and executive director of the Private Eye Writers of America, creator of the Shamus Award, and the cofounder of *Mystery Scene* magazine. He lives in Clarksville, Missouri.

We hope you have enjoyed this Large Print book. Other Thorndike, Wheeler, and Chivers Press Large Print books are available at your library or directly from the publishers.

For information about current and upcoming titles, please call or write, without obligation, to:

Publisher
Thorndike Press
295 Kennedy Memorial Drive
Waterville, ME 04901
Tel. (800) 223-1244

or visit our Web site at:

http://gale.cengage.com/thorndike

OR

Chivers Large Print
published by BBC Audiobooks Ltd
St James House, The Square
Lower Bristol Road
Bath BA2 3SB
England
Tel. +44(0) 800 136919
email: bbcaudiobooks@bbc.co.uk
www.bbcaudiobooks.co.uk

All our Large Print titles are designed for easy reading, and all our books are made to last.